MAIDS

AN EROTIC ANTHOLOGY

MAIDS

AN EROTIC ANTHOLOGY

The Erotic Print Society would like to thank the following, without whose generous help this book would not have been possible:

Henri Breton, China Hamilton, Sylvie Jones, Lynn Paula Russell, Tom Sargent, Clarion Publishing, John DuPret, Linda DuPret, Ben Westwood and Eric Wilkins

London 2005

THE *Erotic* Print Society
Email: eros@eroticprints.org
Web: www.eroticprints.org

ISBN: 1-904989-09-8

Printed and bound in Spain by IGOL S.A., Barcelona, Spain

The Erotic Print Society is a publisher of fine art, photography and fiction books and limited editions. To find out more please visit us on the web at www.eroticprints.org or call us for a catalogue (UK only) on 0871 7110 134.

MAIDS

AN EROTIC ANTHOLOGY

CONTENTS

FOREWORD

Everybody ought to have a maid,
Someone who you hire when you're short of help
To offer you the sort of help
You never get from a spouse:
Fluttering up the stairway,
Shuttering up the windows,
Cluttering up the bedroom,
Buttering up the master,
Puttering all around the house!
Oh, oh, wouldn't she be delicious,
Tidying up the dishes,
Neat as a pin.
Oh, oh, wouldn't she be delightful,
Sweeping out,
Sleeping in.

Stephen Sondheim
A Funny Thing Happened on the Way to the Forum

The young servant was "mighty pretty," wrote Samuel Pepys wistfully, and it was not long before his wife "did find me embracing the girl con my hand sub su coats."

The idea of getting someone to do the menial tasks while you went about your more important business or led a more relaxing life is not new, but by the end of the 17th century a young servant girl was at least getting paid, although three pounds a year was an average wage. Even though she had more choices in life than her ancient Roman antecedents, tuppence a day still seems small recompense for being groped by a randy employer even if it was the famous diarist. When the mistress of the house found out, you were still unceremoniously sacked. Not fucked once, but twice.

Young Griet, the serving girl in Tracy Chevalier's *Girl with a Pearl Earring*, occupied a similarly difficult position while attempting to satisfy the demands of Vermeer, Mrs. Vermeer, Johannes the butcher and avoiding the attentions of Vermeer's rich and rapacious patron.

If you were unlucky enough to be a male servant in the retinue of the appropriately named Mervyn Touchet, Earl of Castlehaven, you would find yourself with your back to the wall, so keen was he on buggering his footmen. His doughty wife accused Mervyn of rape (on some whim, he held her down while one of his benighted lackeys was ordered to penetrate her) and sodomy. Eventually this menace to butlers was found guilty by a court of his peers, who disliked him far more for being a poof and a Catholic than a rapist and abuser of his servants. He was beheaded on Tower Hill in 1631.

The Age of Reason defined the maid's role more clearly. There were parlour maids, lady's maids, kitchen maids and housemaids, who all came under the stern eye of the housekeeper, an older, more experienced woman whose iron rule was law. Hogarth, Rowlandson and other graphic social commentators would include female servants in their etchings, but almost always in the background. The maid carrying a pie, and spilling most of its contents, in Hogarth's *Noon* is having her breasts felt by a blackamoor. He is also kissing her cheek, and she has a dreamy look about her that could indicate that she is contemplating an early bout of inter-racial sex. But despite these cameo appearances, the maid still has no real identity. She remains a poor, put-upon figure, always there to help in *Madame's* love intrigues, warn her of the approaching

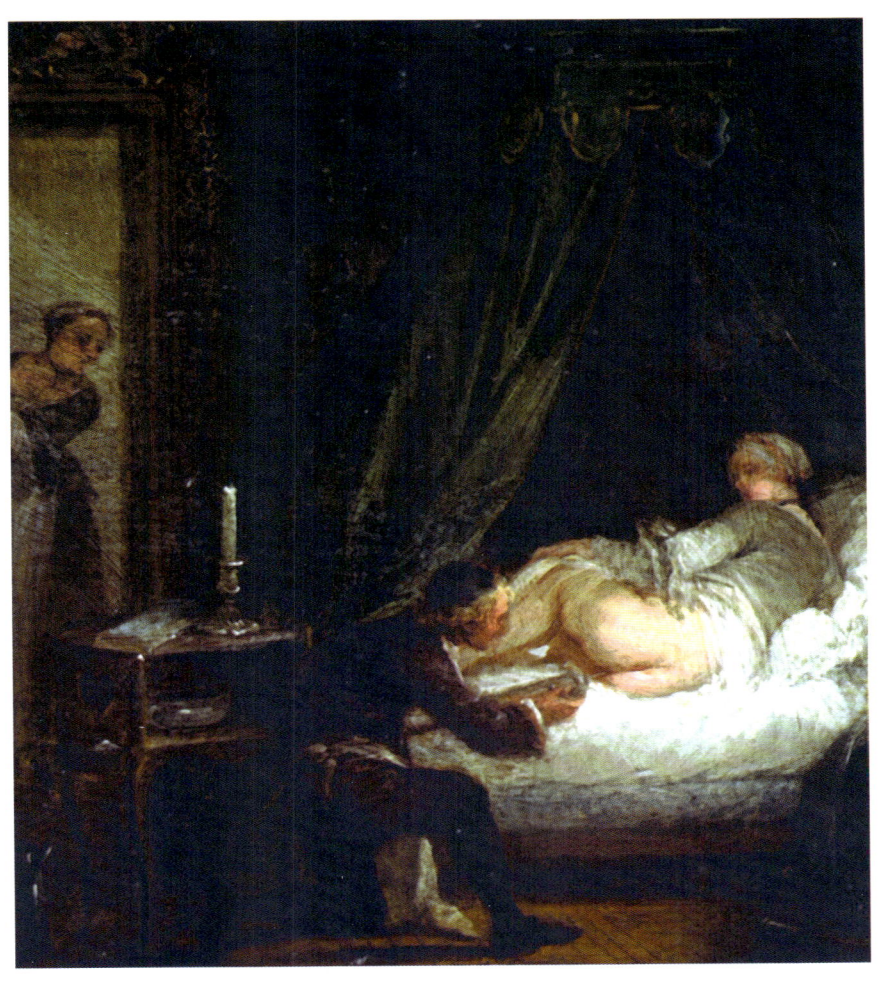

husband or paramour, or administer an enema or douche by means of a large syringe, usually much to the entertainment of a hidden lover.

In those days of Fanny Hill or Tom Jones, with a bit of luck she'd be sleeping, not at the foot of her employers' curtained four-poster as in the century before, but in a poky cupboard at the end of a corridor, a freezing garret or, if she was lucky, by the kitchen range in something like a dog basket. 18th century serving girls weren't meant to have sex. Or if they did, this would not be an erotic event, more a way of relieving sexual tension, a bit of quick coupling to enable the master to lose his sperm. In this century servants were considered dirty, lazy and illiterate, a sub-division of the peasantry. Actresses, nuns, prostitutes and other people's wives were deemed desirable females in the Enlightenment, but not greasy Joan, still keeling her pot.

The serving girl might have languished at this pupal stage unless something had caused metamorphosis. There was a long way to go before she could transform herself into the saucy, provocative fetish-temptress we know and lust after today. She had yet to develop the pantomime, 'allo, 'allo accent that is mandatory for all 'French Maids'. Or her association with the sex industry, either as client's uniformed fantasy or tart's accomplice. She had still to develop to the point where she embodied all of the wildest male sexual fantasies born of the frustrations of a deeply repressed Victorian and Edwardian bourgeoisie. In sharp contrast to the fearsome matriarchs who often ruled the roost, the fantasy maid was sweet, biddable and tractable, an antidote to the twin harridans of mistress and housekeeper.

It wasn't until the Victorian era that the maid would have more than just a walk-on part. Architects were beginning to make allowances for staff rooms in their house plans, if only in the basement or attic, or in a mews, above stables. But if her accommodation was becoming more comfortable, the maid's life was growing more regulated, her existence more precarious and her person more exploited than ever. Even in Edwardian times she was expected to work a 100-hour week with holidays, if any, at her employers' discretion. And gradually, thanks to male attention, she was developing a 'saucy' reputation. Maids were simply considered fair game and expected to be available, not just for randy, Pepysian employers and their sons, but also their male colleagues behind the green baize door, from butler to boot boy. The mistress and housekeeper would be on the lookout for such fun and games and do their best to prevent any philandering, but not always successfully. What was patently unfair was the peremptory manner in which a maid was cast out into the world if she became pregnant – or even caught out 'having connections'.

Dismissal for getting pregnant was a double bind for the unhappy girls. Not only did their condition render them unsuitable for the hard work that a Victorian household required, but they were invariably sent away in disgrace and without a reference. This was tantamount to being sentenced to a term in the workhouse. And it often seemed the lesser of two evils to go 'on the game' than face the penal regime of that institution. One of the 19th century's ironies was that many Victorian do-gooders and feminists saw domestic service as an answer to the plight of young single girls. It was, in fact, one of the main sources of prostitution. Gradually a link between domestic service and prostitution was forged. Prostitution was too close to the bone for ribaldry of the music hall variety – there was an army of sad 'gay' women out there, riddled with disease and in league with the underworld so feared by the Victorian middle classes. But men from every level of society would leer and wink at the mention of a maid in her smart black dress and frilly white cap and apron. They were well aware of the double standard that existed over this job and were only too happy to make their own contribution towards it.

Thus the ethos of the time dictated that these respectable, hard-working young women should avoid being chased upstairs, and do their best to be chaste downstairs. They should hang on to their virtue, maintain a sense of humour and yet retain a certain pert sauciness. All of the maids. The innocent, blushing young skivvy of a between-maid serving out her apprenticeship. The nubile, slightly less innocent housemaid. The floury, perspiring, but still fragrant, kitchen maid. The buxom parlour maid, straightening the fish knives and answering the door. The cheerful chambermaid, plumping the pillows and whisking the bed sheets. The prim but knowing lady's maid, whose precursor, the handmaiden, had poured asses' milk into Cleopatra's bath and anointed her with fragrant oils.

Because of better architectural planning of private houses and vast urban expansion, there was a huge increase in the number of servants living in households in England and Wales. The number of servants rose from 847,000 in 1851 to 1.3 million in 1881. The number of general female servants rose by 33 per cent during the same period. The number of people of both sexes employed as servants was approximately the same as the number of people employed in agriculture.

If you walked down a London street during the second half of the 19th century, theoretically every tenth woman you met would be in domestic service. The exploits of *My Secret Life's* author, Walter, explain just how many opportunities there were to tempt and seduce the vulnerable housemaid:

The abstinence from women for ten days, and the excitement of the last two days, had put me into this state; so directly I saw Bates alone, I thought of her cunt – and how to get into it.

'It's a long time since I gave you a kiss,' said I. Her demure face broke into a smile and she looked all round the room.

'Mrs. Fitzgerald will hear you,' said she (it was my cousin's name). I gave her rosy lips a kiss, and pinched her bum, making some

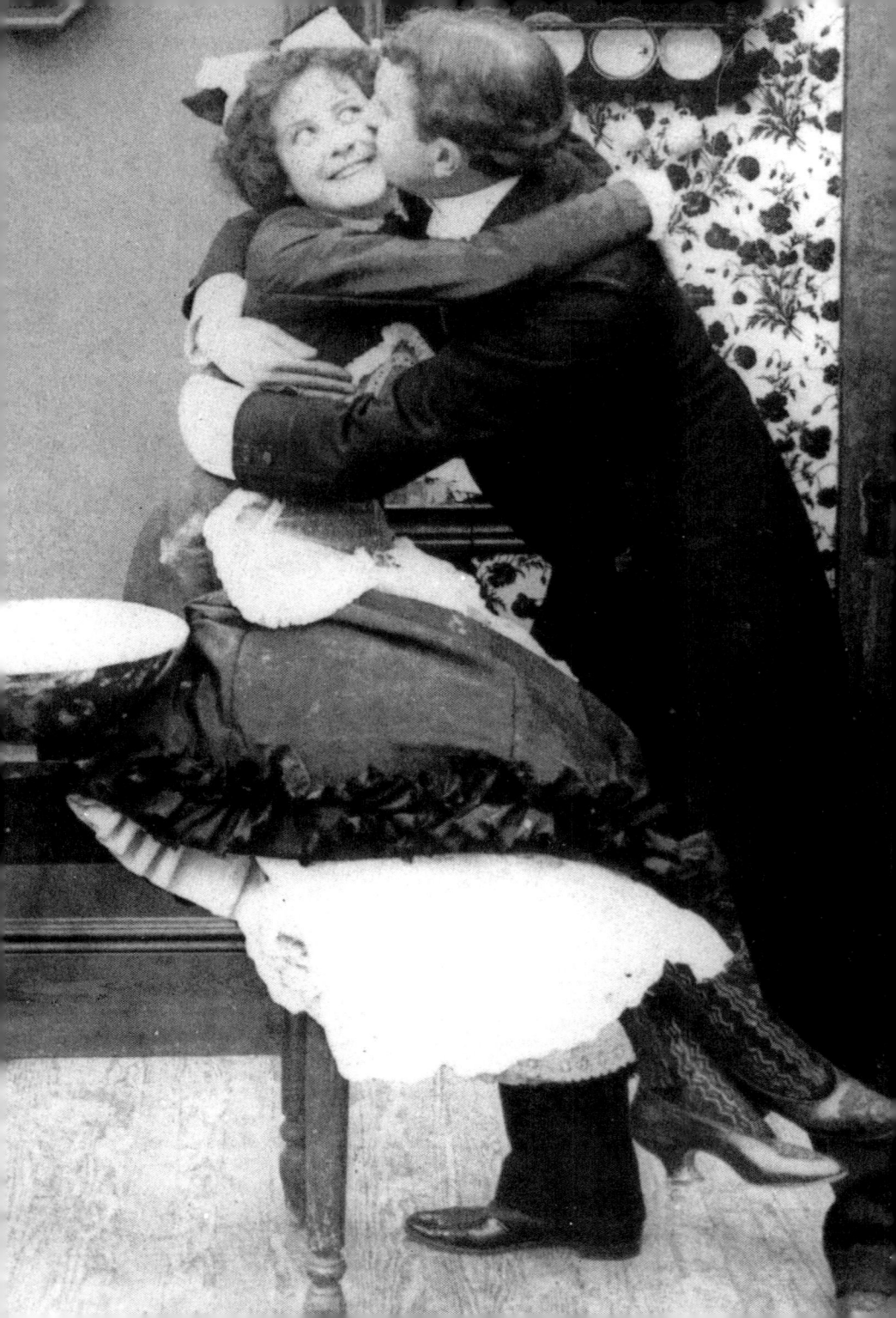

impudent remark. She scuffled but I got her to kiss me, and for a few minutes, this game was carried on.

The bum pinching upset her most.

'Oh, law, don't. You'll make me lose my place, if any ones come in. Oh, if she be coming down, oh, don't, you hurt.'

'I'll pinch it in front then.' Whereon she opened the door wide, I walked into the garden smoking a cigar, for I fancied I heard Hannah coming; but I saw plainly that I might have much fun, if not fucking, with Bates – demure as she looked, and even tho she was going to be married.

Bates had been a long time in my aunt's service. When I had seen her before, I kissed her - but was not encouraged to proceed further; and two years had elapsed since then. My aunt had remarked that she was engaged to be married; that and her demure look, and the difficulties in the way, made me dismiss all idea of getting into her – and had I not had my rutting fever on, dare say should never have attempted it. Now I was in my reckless mood and, having kissed and bum pinched, saw she was not annoyed but only timid. In the dining room I whispered, as she laid luncheon cloth, that I meant to sleep with her.

'I mean to see what color it is,' said I, at which she looked funny but very serious, and eyed me a long time without making any reply.

At every opportunity – and I made many during the day, Hannah being so much with her mother – I attacked her. When she opened the door I kissed her. She was sent to me to a summer house (oh those summer houses, how often I have tailed women in them – of which I shall have to tell more) to say my aunt would be glad to see me. There I told Bates I had hurt my fingers against her bum, and was sure she was softer in front, and made fucking signs with my fingers. Whilst Hannah, with her dark haired cunt, was opposite to me at dinner, I was wondering what sort of quim the maid had and was taken with a furious letch for the wench and saw that every thing tended to giving me a chance with her.

And if temptation and seduction failed, there was always rape, with a trumped up charge of theft and dismissal as a threat. An employer could also insist that female domestics remain single and married to the job. While poverty, violence and prostitution was a condition of employment for most of the female domestic class, it was frequently the employers who posed an even greater threat.

From this precarious existence, a new Maid arose, one who eventually dealt with her master's little peccadilloes with breezy self-possession, who carved out an identity, who evolved, metamorphosed into a proper person, with a proper profession. 'In service' was a career with a hierarchy that stretched from between-maid to housekeeper. The expression of glum pride of the maids in Bill Brandt's photographs say all. We are here to stay, so take us seriously. We are the Vestal Virgins of the domestic profession, from fifteen-year-old skivvy to battleaxe of an old retainer.

But then came the World Wars. The first decimated the male population and saw recently emancipated women leaving domestic service for a variety of new professions that allowed them greater independence. And electrical household appliances became more efficient and labour saving. The Second World War once more rewove the social fabric, causing the middle classes to become defensive about employing servants that they could, in any case, no longer easily afford. By 1961, only 100,000 or so faithful and now ageing retainers remained in service. The uniformed maid passed into history (unless you counted hotel staff, stripagrams and rubber maids) and the male population heaved a collective, regretful sigh. But it was premature. A new contender for the hired, biddable, tractable and sexually available female had been waiting in the wings all this while and now emerged, resplendent, centre stage – the Secretary.

While the environment had changed the game remained the

same. Although the Housekeeper and the Mistress had been subsumed into the Office Manager, often female, the Master had merely become the Boss. But there were crucial differences.

Although, like the Maid, she had a status that was directly in proportion to the importance of her employer, the Secretary came from any background. She was educated, ambitious to get married, to travel and see the world, to enter into business for herself. And with the advent of white-collar workers unions, militant feminism and constructive dismissal, there ceased to be any real comparison between her lot and that of the maid.

The Maid lingered on, if only in caricature. In 1947 Jean Genet wrote *Les Bonnes* (The Maids). A true-life murder of a mistress by her female employees inspired the larcenous author to explore the sadism and masochism inherent in such a working relationship, taking these themes to their absurd limits. In a connected subculture, Eric Stanton and other 50s and 60s cartoonists of the bizarre began to focus on the Maid as a fetish figure. She became the subject of a remarkable number of sadomasochistic plots that were as inventive as they were surreal. Today you can buy a skimpy 'R U Being Served' costume from Anne Summers or a more fetishistic 'Rubber Maid's Dress' from Skin Two Clothing to indicate your personal sexual preferment at a party or to titillate the jaded appetites of your partner.

It's true that replica Maids exist today, from Columbia, from Poland, from the Philippines. They occupy the corridors of hotels, they commute daily from the suburbs, they do not so much wear a uniform as chime in with the hotel chain's decor. Try pinching their bum and you'll end up with a heavy fine if not a custodial sentence.

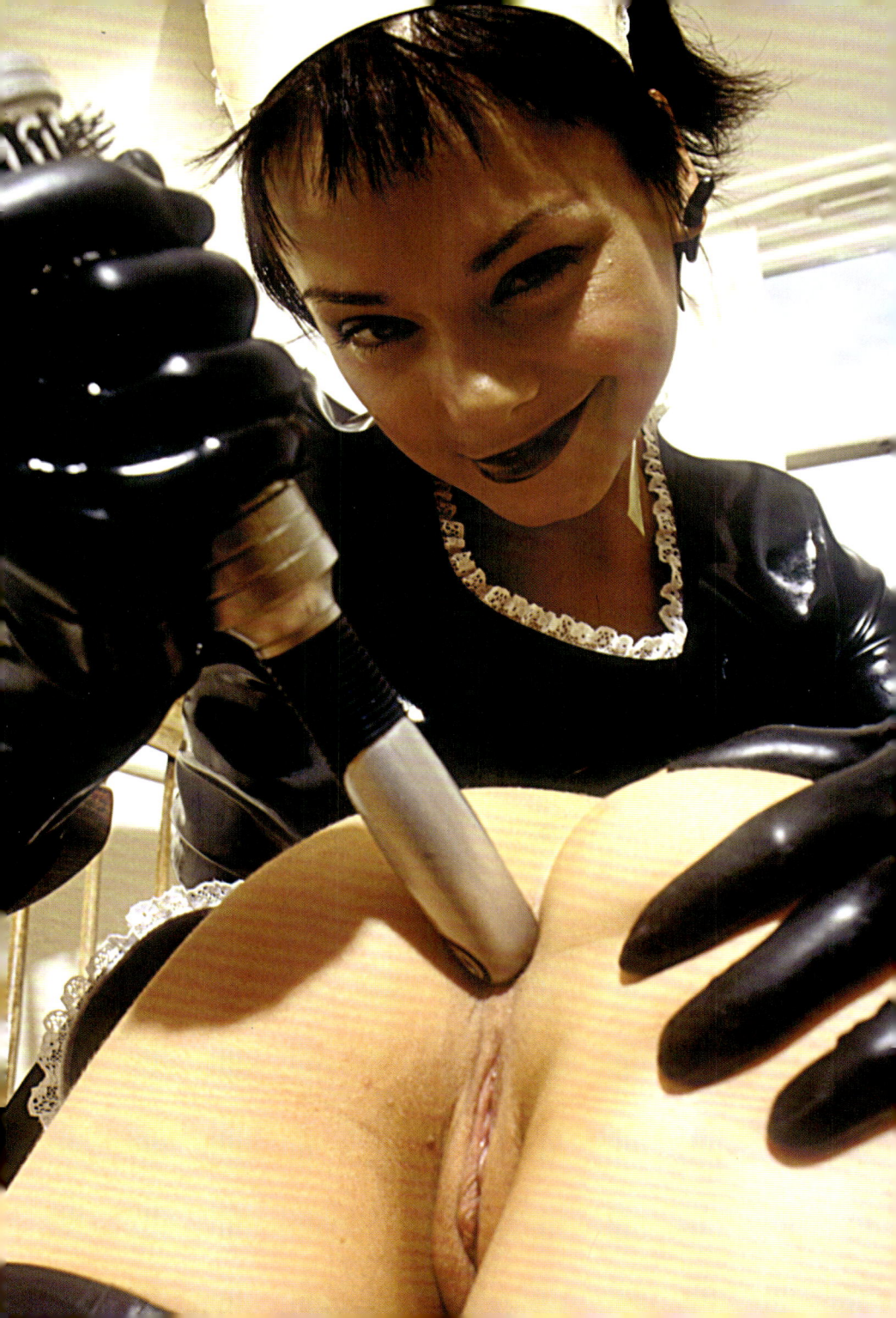

Whoa, the servants they're so helpful, dear
The cook she is a whore
Yes, the butler has a place for her
Behind the pantry door
The Maid, she's French, she's got no sense,
She's wild for Crazy Horse
And when she strips, the chauffeur flips
The footman's eyes get crossed

Don'cha think there's a place for us
Right across the street?
Don'cha think there's a place for you
In between the sheets?

The Rolling Stones
Live with me

GAMIANI

ALFRED DE MUSSET

Our first erotic maid is found in Paris. The year is 1833, the author, Alfred de Musset, sometime lover of Georges Sand, habitué of the most important Parisian literary and artistic salons of the time. De Musset was the author of *Gamiani*, which some say is the fruit of a literary co-operation with Sand, while others point out that it could be a vengeful satire on their affair.

Julie is the redoubtable maid of Countess Gamiani, who is ruthlessly seducing Fanny, *'une jeune personne de qualité'*. Alcide is a young man hoping to gatecrash the party and in doing so, becomes hopelessly enmeshed in the evil Countess' web. No sooner is she supplying her mistress with the milk so stridently requested than she has to deal with the family dog, as well. A maid's work is never done. Despite the weighty classical allusions and the fact that it is largely presented in dramatic form, this is a rollicking good bit of erotic writing. One day, some right-minded person should put it on in the West End as a theatrical endeavour. Although they might encounter difficulties in finding the right pooch to play Medor.

Fanny was so shocked and alarmed that she got up. As for me, I was expecting to see her go off into hysterics. In vain I covered her most delicate parts with kisses. My hands were weary of torturing this unconquerable harpy, for her secreting canals were closed or emptied. I began to draw blood, but the orgasm did not occur.

'I shall leave you now, go to sleep!' she declared.

As she spoke, Gamiani sprang out of bed, opened a door and disappeared from our sight.

'What is it she really wants? Do you know, Fanny?' I asked.

'Hush, Alcide, listen, what cries!' Fanny whispered fearfully. 'She is killing herself. Oh God, the door is locked! Ah, she has gone into Julie's room. Wait a moment, there is a little window over it, and from thence we shall be able to see everything. Let us bring the sofa over there and two chairs. Now get up and let us look.'

And what a sight met our eyes! By the changing flicker of a small candle, the Countess, with her eyes rolled up to the whites, foam on her lips, fluid all down her thighs, was rolling about and groaning on a broad rug made of cats' skins. She was rubbing her back with the greatest agility on the rug. Now and again, the Countess threw her legs up in the air, almost standing thus on her head, showing us her whole back, and then fell back with a forced and nervous laugh.

'Julie,' Gamiani commanded, 'come to me, my head is spinning. Ah, you damned fool, I want to bite you.'

Julie was naked also, but heavily built and very strong. She seized the Countess' hands and feet and bound them together with cords. As the excess of passion was driving her mad, her convulsions made me very anxious. Julie, who seemed absolutely indifferent, was dancing and jumping about like a lunatic, exciting herself at will and, at length having felt the great pleasure of spending, lay back on the armchair. The Countess watched all these movements, and because she could not do the same, could not taste the same delightful intoxication, fell into a renewed rage, twice as terrible as the first. She thought she was a female Prometheus having her heart torn out by a hundred vultures at once.

'Medor! Medor! Come here, take me!' she screamed.

At the sound of his name, an enormous mastiff rushed out from his kennel, and immediately began to lick her clitoris, the tip of which was standing out between her hairs, red and swollen.

The Countess shouted, 'Ah! Ah! Ah!' still more loudly as the pleasure became more intense. One might easily register the degrees of tickling felt by this ungovernable Calymantha.

'Milk, milk! Give me milk!' she gasped.

I was wondering what this cry – such a formidable cry of distress, of agony – meant, when Julie reappeared, armed with an enormous dildo filled with hot milk that had a spring arrangement for spurting the milk ten paces away. With two leather straps, she fitted this ingenious instrument to the right spot on her body. The most bountifully hung stallion, in all his youthful strength, certainly never displayed a more splendid yard (at all events as regards size). I could not imagine it was possible to introduce this great member when, to my great surprise, five or six powerful thrusts, that drew cries of piercing agony from Gamiani, sufficed to push this terrible weapon home to the hilt.

The Countess was suffering hellish torture; she lay stiff and still like the marble statue of Cassandra by Cassini. Julie was sliding it in and out with great regularity and art when Medor, mad at being shoved away, came up behind Julie, whose opened backside displayed a most delicious piece of meat, mounted her suddenly, and got it into her so thoroughly that Julie sank down exhausted in a shower of delight. Such pleasure must indeed be most intense, for it was impossible to imagine a woman enjoying anything as much as she did.

Meanwhile the Countess was swearing vigorously at her own pleasure being interrupted, feeling herself tricked out of coming. But Julie soon came round again, and quickly began to push still more vigorously. As the Countess raised her bottom with a jerk to meet one of her strokes, with her eyes closed and mouth open, Julie saw that the critical instant had arrived and pressed the spring.

'Oh, Oh!' screamed Gamiani. 'Stop, I am melting away, oh, oh, I am spending.'

GALLERY I

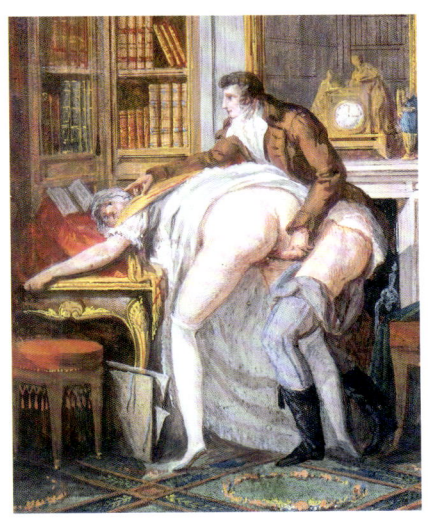

28

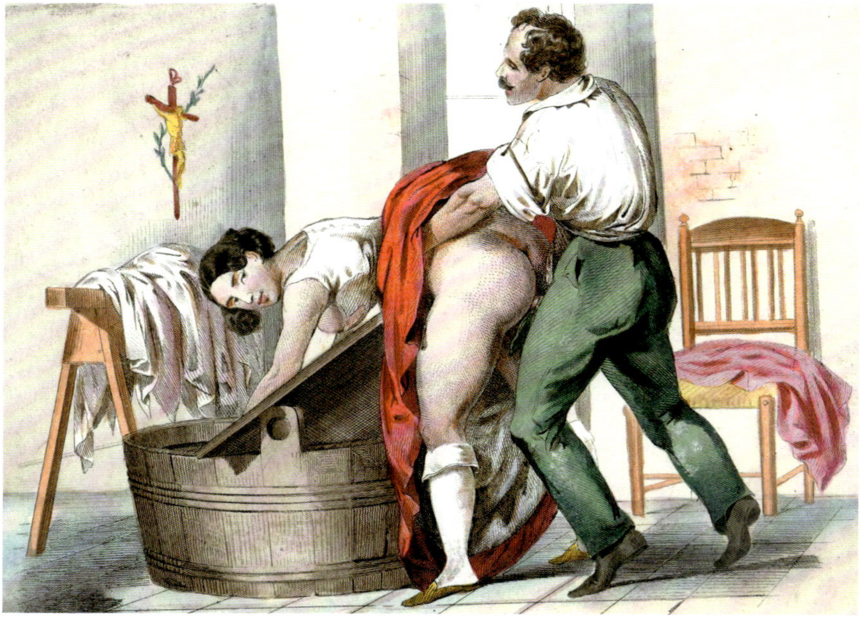

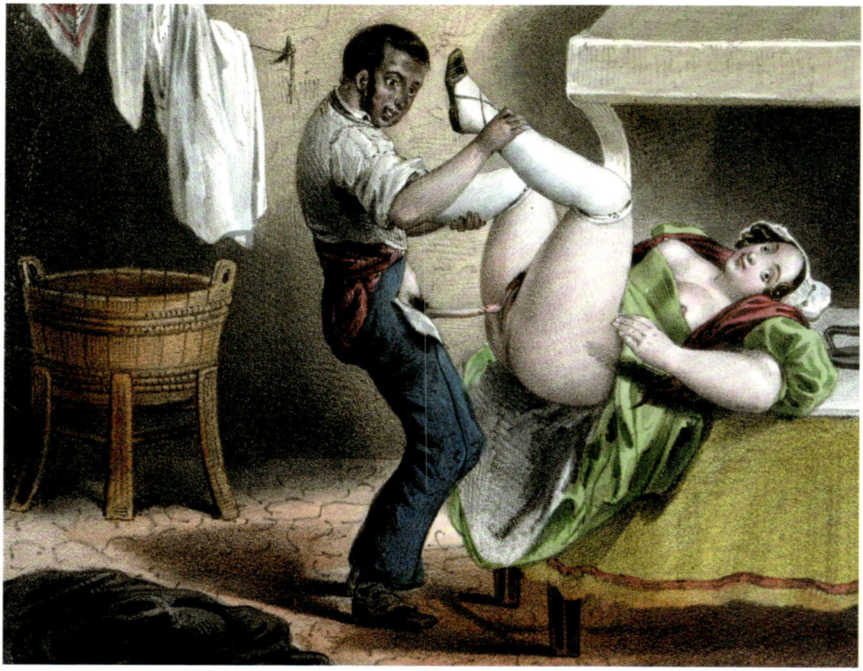

ur̄ jbe précaution

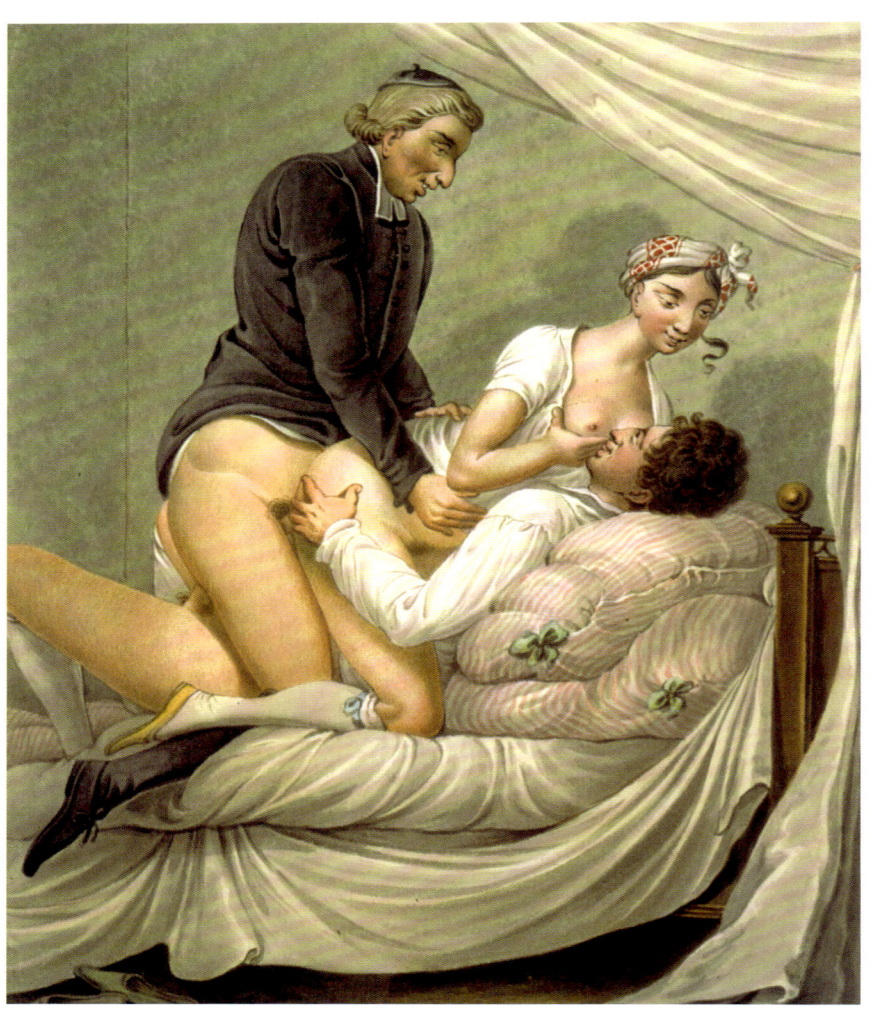

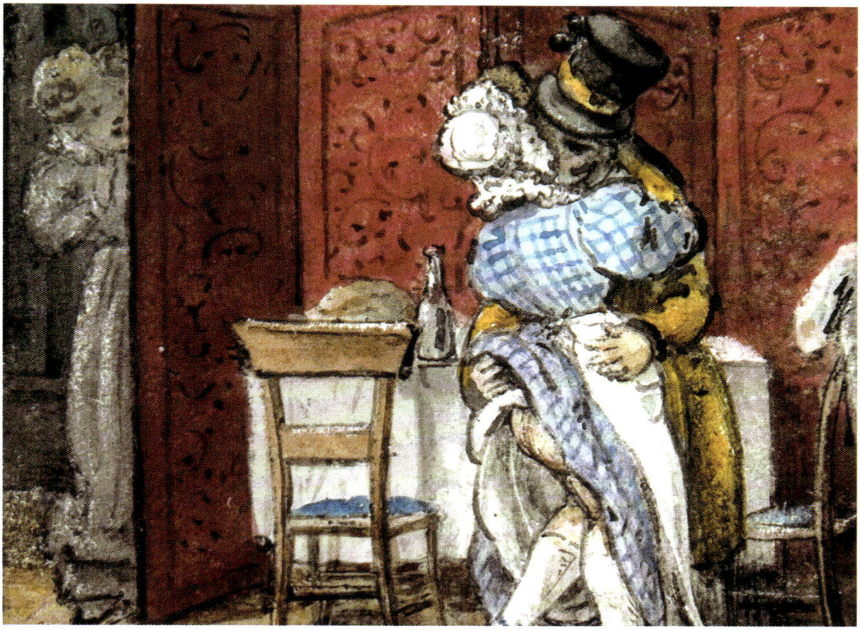

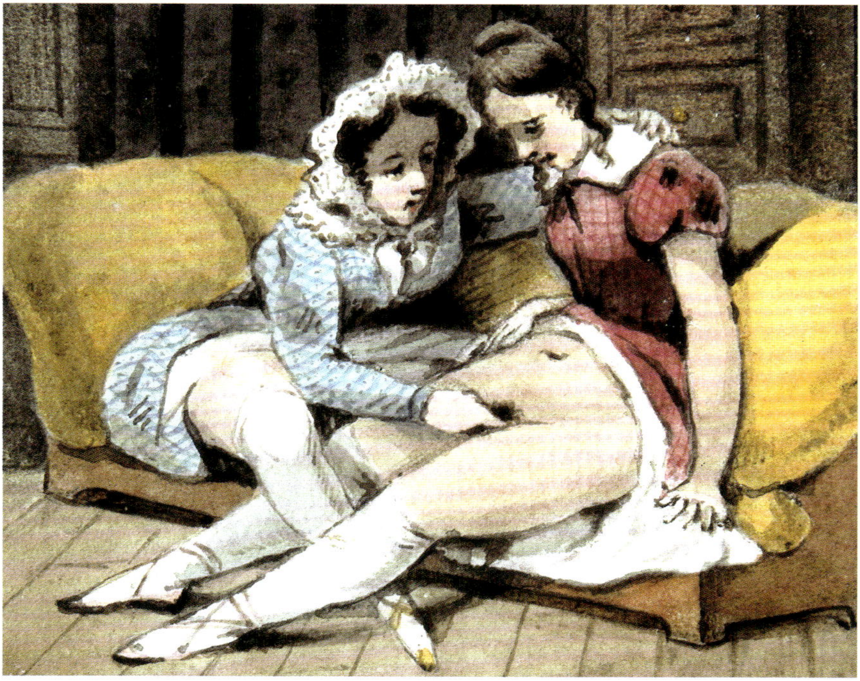

SUMMER IN THE COUNTRY

AUGUSTE POULET-MALASSIS

The author of *A Summer in the Country* (1868), Paul Emmanuel Auguste Poulet-Malassis, was born in 1825. A publisher 'with printer's ink in his blood', since printing was his family's business, Poulet-Malassis published Baudelaire's *Les Fleurs du Mal* and, with Jules Gay, he became one of the most prolific sources of high-class erotica in France during the 1860s. Somehow he found time to write the charming epistolary novel from which the next extract is taken. Albertine, a teacher, writes to Adèle, a former pupil, who is marooned in the countryside for a summer. Adèle writes back to Albertine. Both will become engaged and married during the course of the novel, but that they have been, and still are, bosom friends in more than one sense, soon becomes clear. But for the course of this summer they are separated and must content themselves with writing about, and vicariously sharing, their sexual adventures in the most delicate and circumspect way possible. And so Albertine, the older of our pair of sexual adventuresses, writes to Adèle, telling her of the new maid, Félice, who has arrived at the school where she teaches…

I said just now that school goes on the same as always, neither better nor worse, which is true with regard to the pupils; but among the domestic staff, a new maid arrived a few days ago whom it might be worth taking some trouble over.

Without being exactly pretty, Félice has a very remarkable face. She is twenty four or twenty five years old, small, slender, and a brunette. She comes from Provence. Her hair is very beautiful, she has a slightly aquiline nose, and her eyes, which are grey-blue in colour, are round and large; in fact, they have a rather strange look about them, caused by the dark rings which surround them and her thick black eyebrows, which meet just above the nose. Her upper lip is lined with fine hairs, while a light down, compact and brownish in colour, runs down the side of her cheeks, not unlike the side whiskers of a first year student.

When I tell you that Félice has little white teeth, and dainty hands and feet, you will agree that she is not a girl who should be overlooked. So do not be astonished if I take a shine to her. In fact, I really do intend to give her a try, all that I have lacked so far is an excuse with which to commence hostilities, but I'm busily looking for one. I will keep you posted as to how I get on.

The indisposition of the headmistress, which I mentioned in my last letter, has grown worse and turned into something more serious. She has been in bed for more than a week now, and I have taken over as acting headmistress during that time (quite a promotion). In fact, I'm in sole command here which I don't mind in the least since I have always liked making myself obeyed, as you know.

The headmaster has shown every consideration towards me and has been most courteous.

Farewell. If you see anything else of note from your eerie, don't fail to tell me: I would hate my education to suffer. As for me, remember my promises to you.

Love and kisses,
Albertine

Letter VIII: Adèle to Albertine
B—.
22nd May, 18—

My dearest Albertine,
Our solitude has been invaded: we have had a stream of

visitors from Paris. You would hardly recognise B— any more, everything is so topsy-turvy.

First it was the turn of Maître J—, one of the most famous barristers in Paris, who won an important case for my uncle last year. He's very rich, or so they say. In appearance, he's a small man in his forties, somewhat solemn and preoccupied, who invariably wears a white tie. He has a deep voice, large eyes, a pimply complexion, and is in proud possession of six strands of hair which he combs forwards from the back of his neck over his head.

We've put him up in the guest-room. I must admit that this is rather an anti-climax as far as my right hand peephole is concerned, for I have no intention whatsoever of investigating what our pompous barrister does in the privacy of his chamber. And since he's here for the entire month, you will understand the adverse effect that his presence might have on my studies!

But we also have a young couple staying with us who were only married earlier this year. They are like a pair of turtle doves and I would very much have approved of them as my neighbours, at least I would have been sure of learning something. I did my best to arrange matters in their favour, but my aunt would have none of it: the barrister's greater status was undeniable, and with it went the best room.

We have also been honoured by the visit of a well known author and playwright. His plays are said to be very witty. I hope this is true – in any event they can hardly be less witty than his conversation. What a dull and tiresome individual!

And we are expecting more visitors yet! There is talk of a garden party, picnics, excursions in the countryside, and a boating trip. The Seine is almost next door to us. There has also been mention made of amateur theatricals. You cannot imagine how happy this makes me! I tell you, this summer will really be one to remember!

While waiting for all this to happen, we have organised

some little recitals in the evening. The young bride is an excellent musician, while her husband always puts in a spirited performance, even if he's unlikely to win any medals for it.

This increase in our numbers has meant that we have had to take on more servants. One of the new recruits turned up at the door only this morning. I suspect that she represents a striking contrast to the Félice on whom you wish to slake your evil designs. Here is her description.

She comes from Normandy, and she is blonde, barely eighteen years old, and is even taller than my aunt (who, you will remember, is by no means short for a woman herself). But how perfectly proportioned she is with it! She is all curves, a complete superabundance of flesh!

And that's not all: just imagine that this formidable body is surmounted by a round, cherubic little face, with perfectly clear eyes and an almost childlike expression. In short, she's got a real baby face!

You ought to see the lust in their eyes when the men – masters and servants alike – turn their gaze on her.

Even Maître J— has quite cast off his inexorable gravity. At the sight of our young Normandy lass's dazzling freshness and sumptuous charms, his great eyes opened wide and glowed as bright as burning embers, the colour of his nose deepened from red to crimson, and his six strands of hair positively bristled.

I have no idea what will come of all this, but I fear for Mademoiselle Rose's virtue. It will certainly be subject to some outrageous liberties. As from this moment, I shall not let her out of my sight, and I have no doubt that I shall have some more news for you before very long.

As for you, my dearest Albertine, I wish you every success in the siege you are about to undertake. Above all, keep me informed of how you get on.

Your own,
Adèle

Letter IX: Albertine to Adèle
Paris.
26th May, 18—

My darling little Adèle,

The siege here has been of rather shorter duration than that at Troy. I am mistress of the situation, and the position which you left vacant three months ago has now been filled.

And now you'd like the details, I expect.

This is how I arranged my artillery. Yesterday morning, when I went to visit the headmistress, whose condition is worsening daily, I complained of a slight indisposition. By lunch time the pain had become much worse without, as you might imagine, me being able to offer any precise indications as to the nature of the problem: sometimes it was a headache, sometimes it was nerves. Oh, yes, the nerves – especially the nerves!

That evening I was due to sit up with the headmistress, as I do every night, but I soon felt so unwell that her husband had to insist that I took myself off to bed, offering to keep his wife company himself, and instructing Félice, whose room is quite close to mine, to keep a watchful eye on me.

This was exactly what I had been planning. I got up with a little sigh and made my way, a trifle groggily, towards my bedroom, with my favourite chambermaid in tow.

By the time I got there I was so prostrate that I had to be helped to undress. After I'd had a cup of camomile tea in bed, I was feeling much better though, and I sent Félice off to tell my employer's husband that he was not to worry on my account, since I had recovered from my indisposition and all I needed was a good night's rest.

Once I was satisfied that everything was safe from this direction and the messenger had returned safely, I suffered another attack. Having been rather a vague sort of ailment until this moment, my indisposition now made up its mind that it was a nervous problem, and I waved my arms about and writhed around in my bed as appropriate. Félice, completely bewildered by this stage, had just suggested that she should fetch the headmistress's husband when, amazingly enough, the attack suddenly came to an end. As a result, she decided to spend the night with me, and drew up a chair by the side of the bed.

After an uneventful quarter of an hour, I suggested that she should go back to her own room. Naturally, she declined. The upshot of this was that, to salve her conscience, I told her that I would allow her to share my bed with me; that way, if a fresh attack came on, she would be there to help me.

After some humming and hawing, she made up her mind to accept this proposition.

The critical moment was at hand.

There was my Félice taking off her dress, petticoat, and corset, while I watched everything out the corner of my eye; as she removed her garments one by one, I discovered just how gracious and pure was her body, though still that of an adolescent.

Finally, she got into bed!

Once I felt her next to me, my whole body was gripped by a kind of fever. In consequence of having pretended to be sick, I had almost become ill in earnest. The strength of my desire for her – for the last week I had observed the strictest continence in expectation of this happy moment – and the fear of rejection, not to mention my apprehensions of the scandal which might result, combined to produce such a shock to my nervous system that my teeth began to chatter and I was wracked by a trembling fit that I was powerless to control.

In fact, my darling Adèle, it could be said that I played my role to perfection.

First, I asked Félice to put out the candle because, I said, the light prevented me from sleeping.

After this precaution had been effected, and I had allowed

five minutes to pass by (five centuries more like!), and unable to restrain myself any longer, I turned towards her, with a deep sigh. She asked me whether I was suffering.

'Terribly, my dear,' I replied.

Then, suddenly pouncing on her, I threw my arms around her neck, as if begging for help, and hugged her to me.

This advance did not meet with the hostile reception I had anticipated; on the contrary, I thought that I detected a slight pressure in response to my own. The young girl would have done anything to relieve my suffering!

Encouraged by this opening move, and my appetite further whetted by an early success, I pinioned her tightly in my arms, still groaning and complaining about the wretched state of my nerves. Then, with a cautious hand, for I had no wish to alarm her, I began to explore her body, which I soon discovered was as fresh, supple and enticing as I had imagined and that her skin was delicate and soft.

Encountering no resistance, and feeling that I was being encouraged rather than repulsed, I decided to attempt a major advance. I slipped my left arm around Félice, pressed my lips against hers while, forcing her knees apart, I slid my right hand gently between her velvety thighs which, far from trying to arrest my progress, seemed positively to anticipate my every move.

By now I was almost at my goal – almost! Suddenly, I pulled back my hand and let out an exclamation of surprise to which my Provençal girl reacted with a long peal of hysterical laughter.

I can imagine your amazement at this moment! You must be wondering what on earth could have stopped me in my tracks like that, especially such pretty tracks as these? Why the laughter? Why my dismay? In your last letter you mention a certain pubic fleece, well known to both of us, 'whose graceful curls had been coquettishly trimmed...' Well, my dear girl, if what you referred to could be called a fleece, what might you possibly call what I had just felt? At the very least I must have stumbled on a forest, perhaps not as virgin as those to be found in the Americas, but almost as impenetrable. Or rather – no, let's not go groping after unlikely metaphors. Very well, call it a fleece if you will, a veritable fleece: bushy, bristling, tangled, rough and unkempt to the touch. It was more like a goatskin of the kind Jacob covered himself with to trick good old Isaac, which made me think, incidentally, that the tribe of Esau is by no means extinct. There could be no doubt about it: Félice must descend directly from the line of the hairy patriarch who was so partial to lentils.

But to get back to my story.

When Félice's laughter had died down, and I had recovered from my shock, the wicked girl confessed to me that for the last quarter of an hour or more she had guessed what I was up to and had not been in the least taken in by my attack of nerves. Nonetheless, she had let me play my hand right to the end, being curious to know what effect it would have on me when I put my hand on the strange shock of hair which adorns her body. The result had been worth waiting for.

Thinking back over the yelp I had so naturally let out and the abrupt way I had withdrawn my hand, we both began to laugh uncontrollably, and the closest and most good-humoured friendship was established between us as a result. Félice took hold of my hand, which was still rather hesitant, and took me on a conducted tour of those dense thickets that I could still only penetrate after some effort. She soon proved to me by her transports of delight – as intense as they were often repeated, that she was no less devoted than I am to those pleasures which had involved me in so much unnecessary diplomatic activity.

In short, we were extremely pleased with each other and we spent the rest of the night in gainful employment. When, the next morning, the headmistress and her husband enquired whether I had recovered from my indisposition, they concluded from the dark rings under my eyes and from the tired look on my face that I must have slept badly, and they extended their sympathy to me.

Well, I've kept my word, as you can see. That's the story of my latest conquest down to the last detail. Now it's your turn.

Devil take that wretched little lawyer of yours! What business was it of his to turn up like that and ruin a   perfectly good lesson in Natural History which could have proved so instructive? And right from the start, too! Fortunately, the resources offered by B— are more than a match for the likes of him.

Goodbye for the present, my darling Adèle. I send you my hugs and kisses. Remember I shall always love you, despite my flagrant infidelity.

Your very own,

Albertine

GALLERY II

le chasse mouches

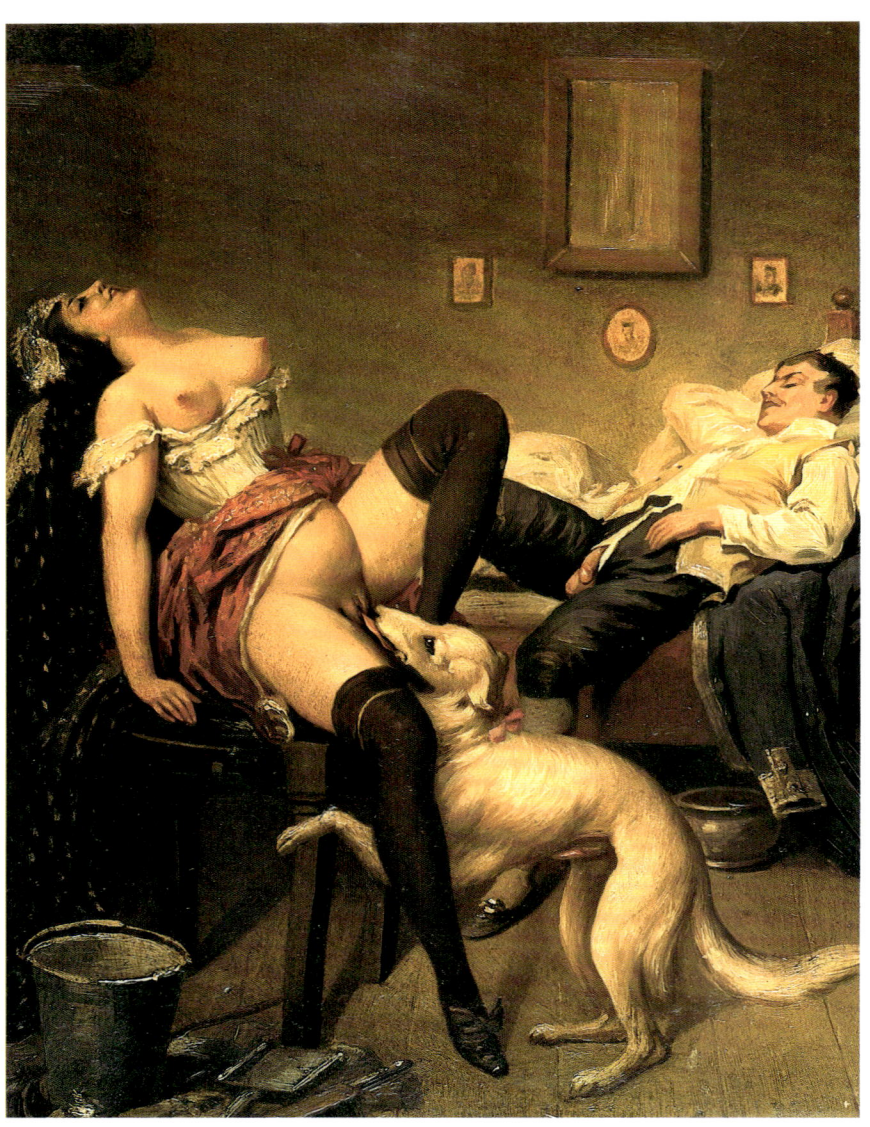

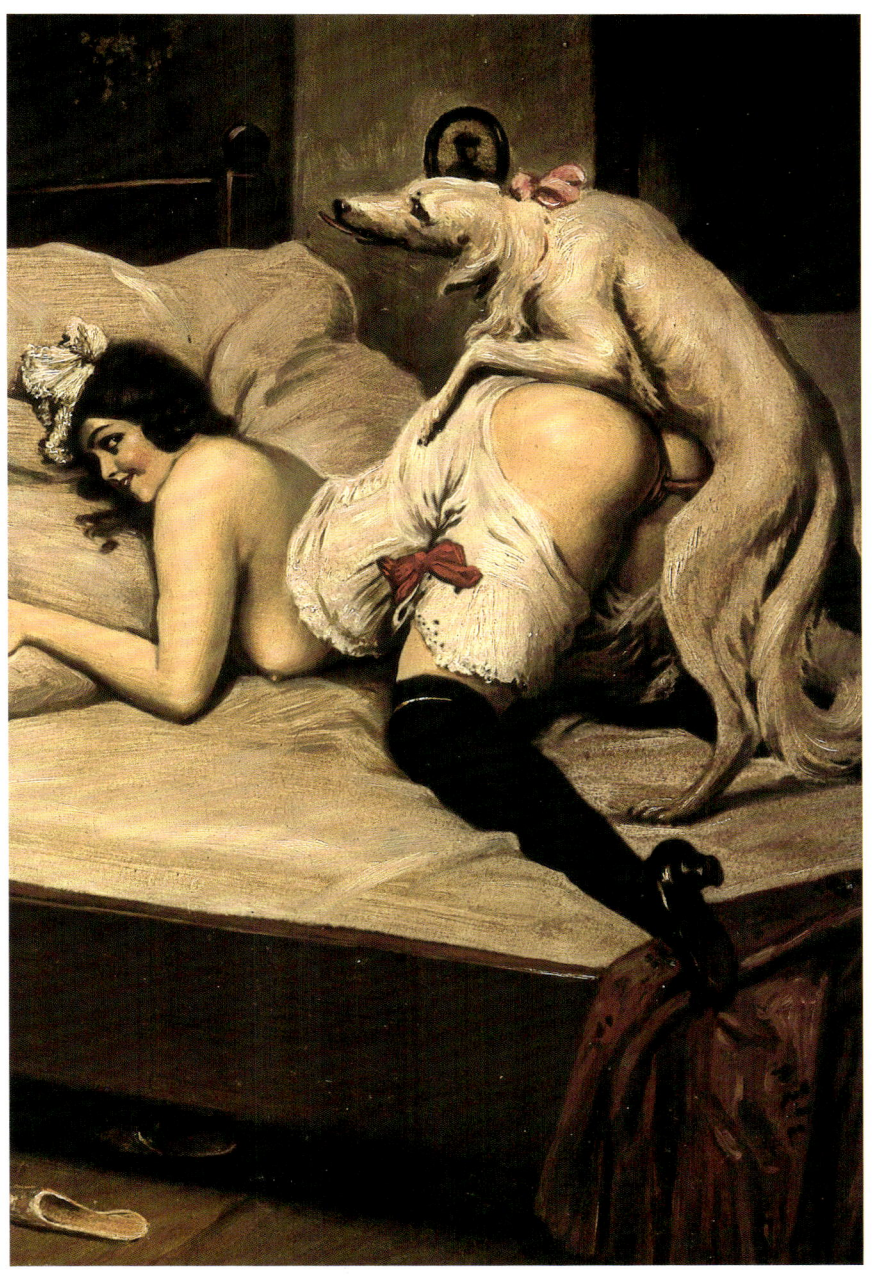

LADY POKINGHAM

ANONYMOUS

Lady Pokingham, or *They All Do It* was first published in *The Pearl*, subtitled *A Monthly Journal of Facetiæ and Voluptuous Reading*, which appeared between July 1879 and December 1880.

Lady P. has stood the test of time. Beatrice Pokingham is a true Victorian porn queen, heroically fornicating her way through life in a way that is positively nymphomaniac. There is the inevitable Victorian obsession with flagellation, but this she takes in her stride. The anonymous author has given her an appetite and stamina for sexual encounters that never flags until she (literally) drops dead. This great erotic heroine becomes more than two-dimensional, and once encountered, is never forgotten. There's also a couple of amusing literary references: Disraeli's *Lothair* is parodied and a passage from Alfred de Musset's *Gamiani* is also 'borrowed' to good effect. At times, the language is surprisingly contemporary in feel, with 'pussy' making an early and very determined appearance. 'Below stairs' is not neglected either, as the following passage will tell. Here young Lucy, 'one of the prettiest housemaids', and the butler, William, unwittingly treat Alice, a young school friend of Lady Pokingham, to an utterly depraved (and highly instructive) display of lovemaking. One thing leads to another, and before long the eager ingénue is thoroughly and delightfully corrupted.

Up betimes next day she told her lady's-maid she was going to enjoy the fresh air in the garden before breakfast, and then hurried off to her place of observation, scrambled through the window regardless of dirt and dust, took off her boots as soon as she alighted in the disused passage and silently crept up to the glass door, but to her chagrin found the panes so dirty as to be impervious to sight; however, she was so far lucky as to find a fine large keyhole quite clear, and two or three cracks in the woodwork, so that she could see nearly every part of the place, which was full of light from a skylight overhead. Mr William was not there, but soon made his appearance, bringing a great basket of plate, which had been used the previous day, and for a few minutes was really busy looking in his pantry book, and counting spoons, forks, &c., but was soon finished, and began to look at a little book, which he took from a drawer. Just then, Lucy, one of the prettiest housemaids, a dark beauty of about eighteen, entered the room without ceremony, saying, 'Here's some of your plate off the sideboard. Where's your eyes, Mr William, not to gather up all as you ought to do?' William's eyes seemed to beam with delight as he caught her round the waist, and gave her a luscious kiss on her cheek, saying: 'Why, I keep them for you, dear, I knew you would bring the plate'; then showing the book, 'What do you think of that position, dear? How would you like it so?' Although pleased, the girl blushed up to the roots of her hair as she looked at the picture. The book dropped to the floor, and William pulled her on to his knee, and tried to put his hand up her clothes. 'Ah! No! No!' she cried, in a low voice; 'you know I can't today, but perhaps I can tomorrow; you must be good today, sir. Don't stick up your impudent head like that. There – there – there's a squeeze for you; now I must be off,' she said, putting her hand down into his lap, where it could not be seen what she was after. In a second or two she jumped up, and in spite of his efforts to detain her, escaped from the pantry. William, evidently in a great state of excitement, subsided on to a sofa, muttering, 'The little witch, what a devil she is; I can't help myself, but she will be all right tomorrow.' Alice, who was intently observing everything, was shocked and surprised to see his trousers all unbuttoned in front, and a great long fleshy-looking thing sticking out, seemingly hard and stiff, with a ruby-coloured head. Mr William took hold of it with one hand, apparently for the purpose of placing it in his breeches, but he seemed to hesitate, and closing his right hand upon the shaft, rubbed it up and down. 'Ah! What a fool I am to let her excite me so. Oh! Oh! I can't help it; I must.' He seemed to sigh as his hand increased its rapid motion. His face flushed, and his eyes seemed ready to start from his head, and in a few moments something spurted from his instrument, the drops falling over his hands and legs, some even a yard or two over the floor. This seemed to finish his ecstasy. He sank back quite listless for a few minutes, and then rousing himself, wiped his hands on a towel, cleared up every drop of the mess, and left the pantry.

Alice was all over in a burning heat from what she had seen but instinctively felt that the mystery was only half unravelled, and promised herself to be there and see what William and Lucy would do next day. Mr William took her for a walk as usual, and read to her, whilst she sat on his knee, and Alice wondered what could have become of that great stiff thing which she had seen in the morning. With the utmost apparent innocence, her hands touched him casually, where she hoped to feel the monster, but only resulted in feeling a rather soft kind of bunch in his pocket.

Another morning arrived to find Alice at her post behind the disused glass door, and she soon saw Mr William bring in his plate, but he put it aside, and seemed all impatient for Lucy's arrival. 'Ah!' he murmured, 'I'm as stiff as a rolling pin at the very thought of the saucy darling,' but his ideas were cut short by the appearance of Lucy herself, who carefully bolted the door inside. Then rushing into his arms, she covered him with kisses, exclaiming, in a low voice, 'Ah! How I have longed for him these three or four days. What a shame women should be stopped in that way from enjoying themselves once a month. How is he this morning?' as her hands nervously unbuttoned Mr William's trousers, and grasped his ready truncheon.

'What a hurry you are in, Lucy!' gasped her lover, as she almost stifled him with her kisses. 'Don't spoil it all by your impatience; I must have my kiss first.'

With a gentle effort he reclined her backwards on a sofa, and
raised her clothes till Alice had a full view of a splendid pair
of plump, white legs; but what riveted her gaze most was the
luscious looking, pouting lips of Lucy's cunny, quite vermilion
in colour, and slightly gaping open in a most inviting manner,
as her legs were wide apart, and her mons Veneris which was
covered with a profusion of beautiful curly black hair.

The butler was down on his knees in a moment, and glued
his lips to her crack, sucking and kissing furiously, to the infinite
delight of the girl, who sighed and wriggled with pleasure, till at
last Mr William could no longer restrain himself, but getting up
upon his knees between Lucy's legs, he brought his shaft to the
charge, and to Alice's astonishment, fairly ran it right into the
gaping crack, till it was all lost in her belly; they lay still for a few
moments, enjoying the conjunction of their persons, till Lucy
heaved up her bottom, and the butler responded to it by a shove,
then they commenced a more exciting struggle. Alice could see
the manly shaft as it worked in and out of her sheath, glistening
with lubricity, whilst the lips of her cunny seemed to cling to it
each time of withdrawal, as if afraid of losing such a delightful
sugar stick; but this did not last long, their movements got more
and more furious, till at last both seemed to meet in a spasmodic
embrace, as they almost fainted in each other's arms, and Alice
could see a profusion of creamy moisture oozing from the crack
of Lucy, as they both lay in a kind of lethargy of enjoyment after
their battle of love.

Mr William was the first to break the silence: 'Lucy, will you
look in tomorrow, dear; you know that old spy, Mary, will be back
from her holiday in a day or two, and then we shan't often have
a chance.'

Lucy – 'Ah; you rogue, I mean to have a little more now, I
don't care if we're caught; I must have it,' she said, squeezing
him with her arms and gluing her lips to his, as she threw her
beautiful legs right over his buttocks, and commenced the

engagement once more by rapidly heaving her bottom; in fact, although he was a fine man, the weight of his body seemed as nothing in her amorous excitement.

The butler's excuses and pleading of fear, in case he was missed, &c., were all of no avail; she fairly drove him on, and he was soon as furiously excited as herself, and with a profusion of sighs, expressions of pleasure, endearment, &c., they soon died away again into a state of short voluptuous oblivion. However, Mr William was too nervous and afraid to let her lie long; he withdrew his instrument from her foaming cunny, just as it was all slimy and glistening with the mingled juices of their love, but what a contrast to its former state, as Alice now beheld it much reduced in size, and already drooping its fiery head.

Lucy jumped up and let down her clothes, but kneeling on the floor before her lover, she took hold of his limp affair, and gave it a most luscious sucking, to the great delight of Mr William, whose face flushed again with pleasure, and as soon as Lucy had done with her sucking kiss, Alice saw that his instrument was again stiff and ready for a renewal of their joys.

Lucy, laughing in a low tone – 'There, my boy, I'll leave you like that, think of me till tomorrow; I couldn't help giving the darling a good suck after the exquisite pleasure he had afforded me; it's like being in heaven for a little while.'

With a last kiss on the lips, they parted and Mr William again locked his door, whilst Alice made good her retreat to prepare herself for breakfast.

It was a fine warm morning in May, and soon after breakfast Alice, with William for her guardian, set off for a ramble in the park; her blood was in a boil, and she longed to experience the joys she was sure Lucy had been surfeited with; they sauntered down to the lake, and she asked William to give her a row in the boat; he unlocked the boat-house, and handed her into a nice, broad, comfortable skiff, well furnished with soft seats and cushions.

'How nice to be here, in the shade,' said Alice; 'come into the boat, Willie, we will sit in it a little while, and you shall read to me before we have a row.'

'Just as you please, Miss Alice,' he replied, with unwonted deference, stepping into the boat, and sitting down in the stern sheets.

'Ah my head aches a little, let me recline it in your lap,' said Alice, throwing off her hat, and stretching herself along on a cushion. 'Why are you so precise this morning, Willie? You know I don't like to be called Miss, you can keep that for Lucy.' Then noticing his confusion, 'You may blush, sir, I could make you sink into your shoes if you only knew all I have seen between you and Miss Lucy.'

Alice reclined her head in a languid manner on his lap, looking up and enjoying the confusion she had thrown him into; then designedly resting one hand on the lump which he seemed to have in his pocket, as if to support herself a little, she continued: 'Do you think, Willie, I shall ever have as fine legs as Lucy? Don't you think I ought soon to have long dresses, sir! I'm getting quite bashful about showing my calves so much.' The butler had hard work to recover his composure, the vivid recollection of the luscious episode with Lucy before breakfast was so fresh in his mind that Alice's allusions to her, and the soft girlish hand resting on his privates (even although he thought her as innocent as a lamb) raised an utter of desire in his feverish blood, which he tried to allay as much as possible, but little by little the unruly member began to swell, till he was sure she must feel it throb under her hand. With an effort he slightly shifted himself, so as to remove her hand lower down on to the thigh, as he answered as gravely as possible (feeling assured Alice could know nothing): 'You're making game of me this morning. Don't you wish me to read, Alice?"

Alice, excitedly, with an unusual flush on her face – 'You naughty man, you shall tell me what I want to know this time:

How do babies come? What is the parsley bed, the nurses and doctors say they come out of? Is it not a curly lot of hair at the bottom of the woman's belly? I know that's what Lucy's got, and I've seen you kiss it, sir!'

William felt ready to drop; the perspiration stood on his brow in great drops, but his lips refused to speak, and Alice continued in a soft whisper: 'I saw it all this morning, Willie dear, and what joy that great red-head thing of yours seemed to give her. You must let me into the secret, and I will never tell. This is the monster you shoved into her so furiously. I must look at it and feel it; how hard it has got under my touch. La! What a funny thing! I can get it out as Lucy did,' pulling open his trousers and letting out the rampant engine of love. She kissed its red velvety head, saying: 'What a sweet, soft thing to touch. Oh! I must caress it a little.' Her touches were like fire to his senses; speechless with rapture and surprise, he silently submitted to the freak of the wilful girl, but his novel position was so exciting he could not restrain himself, and the sperm boiled up from his penis all over her hands and face.

'Ah!' she exclaimed. 'That's just what I saw it do yesterday morning. Does it do that inside of Lucy?'

Here William recovered himself a little, and wiping her face and hands with his handkerchief, put away the rude plaything, saying, 'Oh! My God! I'm lost! What have you done, Alice? It's awful! Never mention it again. I mustn't walk out with you any more.'

Alice burst into sobs.

'Oh! Oh! Willie! How unkind! Do you think I will tell? Only I must share the pleasure with Lucy. Oh! Kiss me as you did her, and we won't say any more about it today.'

William loved the little girl too well to refuse such a delightful task, but he contented himself with a very short suck at her virgin cunny, lest his erotic passion should urge him to outrage her at once.

'How nice to feel your lovely tongue there. How beautifully it tickled and warmed me all over; but you were so quick, and left off just as it seemed nicer than ever, dear Willie,' said Alice, embracing and kissing him with ardour.

'Gently, darling; you mustn't be so impulsive; it's a very dangerous game for one so young. You must be careful how you look at me, or notice me, before others,' said Mr William, returning her kisses, and feeling himself already quite unable to withstand the temptation of such a delicious liaison.

'Ah!' said Alice, with extraordinary perception for one so young. 'You fear Lucy. Our best plan is to take her into our confidence. I will get rid of my lady's-maid, I never did like her, and will ask mama to give Lucy the place. Won't that be fine, dear? We shall be quite safe in all our little games then.'

The butler, now more collected in his ideas, and with a cooler brain, could not but admire the wisdom of this arrangement, so he assented to the plan, and he took the boat out for a row to cool their heated blood, and quiet the impulsive throbbings of a pair of fluttering hearts.

The next two or three days were wet and unfavourable for outdoor excursions, and Alice took advantage of this interval to induce her mother to change her lady's-maid, and install Lucy in the situation.

Alice's attendant slept in a little chamber, which had two doors, one opening into the corridor whilst the other allowed free and direct access to her little mistress's apartment, which it adjoined.

The very first night Lucy retired to rest in her new room, she had scarcely been half an hour in bed (where she lay, reflecting on the change, and wondering how she would now be able to enjoy the butler's company occasionally), before Alice called out for her. In a moment she was at the young lady's bedside, saying: 'What can I do, Miss Alice, are you not warm enough? These damp nights are so chilly.'

'Yes, Lucy,' said Alice, 'that must be what it is. I feel cold and restless. Would you mind getting in bed with me? You will soon make me warm.'

Lucy jumped in, and Alice nestled close up to her bosom, as if for warmth, but in reality to feel the outlines of her beautiful figure.

'Kiss me, Lucy,' she said; 'I know I shall like you so much better than Mary. I couldn't bear her.' This was lovingly responded to, and Alice continued, as she pressed her hand on the bosom of her bedfellow, 'What large titties you have, Lucy. Let me feel them. Open your nightdress, so I can lay my face against them.'

The new *femme de chambre* was naturally of a warm and loving disposition; she admitted all the familiarities of her young mistress, whose hands began to wander in a most searching manner about her person, feeling the soft, firm skin of her bosom, belly, and bottom; the touches of Alice seemed to fire the blood, and rouse every voluptuous emotion within her; she sighed and kissed her little mistress again and again.

Alice – 'What a fine rump! How hard and plump your flesh is, Lucy! Oh, my! what's all this hair at the bottom of your belly? My dear, when did it come?'

Lucy – 'Oh! pray don't, miss, it's so rude; you will be the same in two or three years' time; it frightened me when it first began to grow, it seemed so unnatural.'

Alice – 'We're only girls, there is no harm in touching each other, is there; just feel how different I am.'

Lucy – 'Oh! Miss Alice,' pressing the young girl's naked belly to her own, 'you don't know how you make me feel when you touch me there.'

Alice (with a slight laugh) – 'Does it make you feel better when Mr William, the butler, touches you, dear?' tickling the hairy crack with her finger.

Lucy – 'For shame, miss! I hope you don't think I would let

him touch me' – evidently in some confusion.

Alice – 'Don't be frightened, Lucy, I won't tell, but I have seen it all through the old glass door in his pantry. Ah! you see I know the secret, and must be let in to share the fun.'

Lucy – 'Oh! My God! Miss Alice, what have you seen? I shall have to leave the house at once.'

Alice – 'Come, come, don't be frightened, you know I'm fond of Mr William, and would never do him any harm, but you can't have him all to yourself; I got you for my maid to prevent your jealous suspicions and keep our secret between us.'

Lucy was in a frightful state of agitation. 'What! has he been such a brute as to ruin you, Miss Alice! I'll murder him if he has,' she cried.

Alice – 'Softly, Lucy, not so loud, someone will hear you; he's done nothing yet, but I saw your pleasure when he put that thing into your crack, and am determined to share your joys, so don't be jealous, and we can all three be happy together.'

Lucy – 'It would kill you, dear, that big thing of his would split you right up.'

Alice – 'Never mind,' kissing her lovingly, 'you keep the secret and I'm not afraid of being seriously hurt.'

Lucy sealed the compact with a kiss, and they spent a most loving night together, indulging in every variety of kissing and tickling, and Alice had learnt from her bedfellow nearly all the mysterious particulars in connection with the battles of Venus before they fell asleep in each other's arms.

Fine weather soon returned, and Alice, escorted by the butler, went for one of her usual rambles, and they soon penetrated into a thick copse at the further end of the park, and sat down in a little grassy spot, where they were secure from observation.

GALLERY III

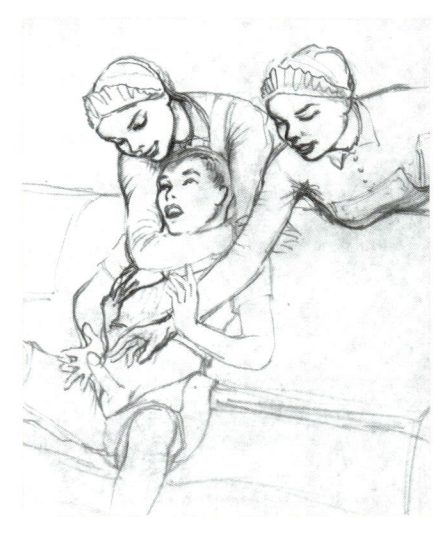

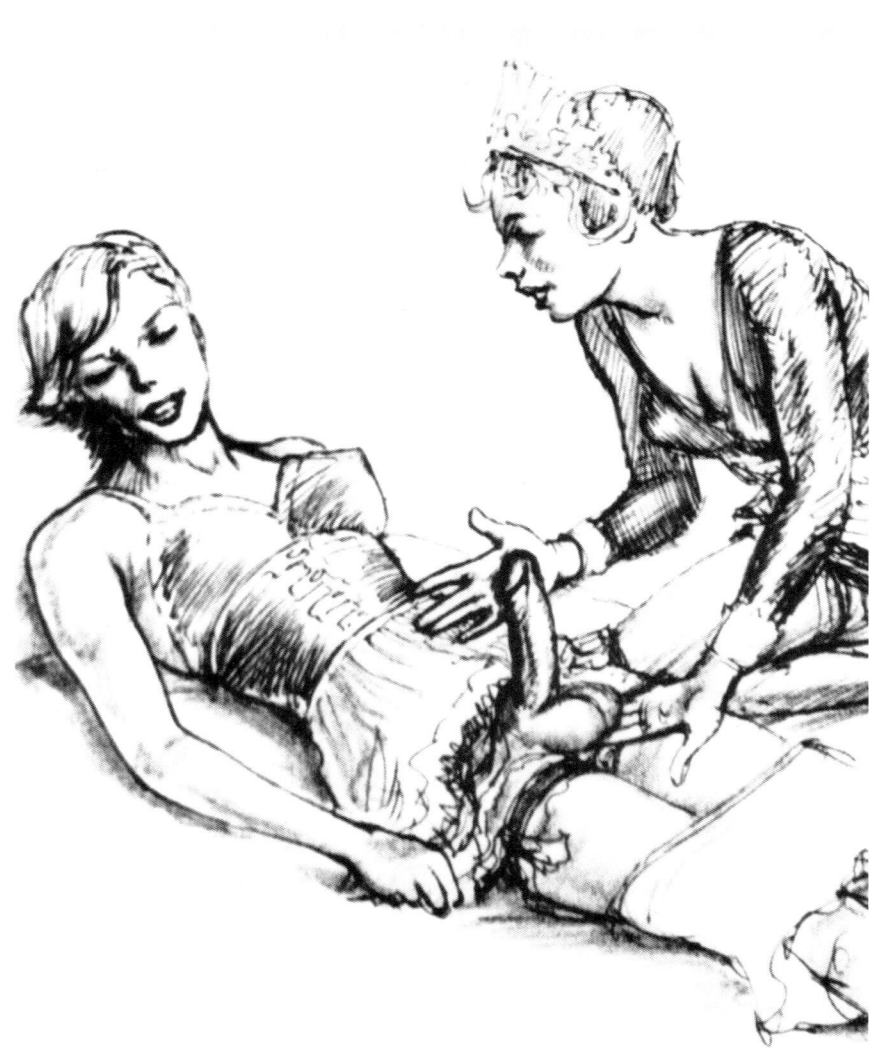

Henry, how long does it take you to put that cat out

AN EXTRACT FROM

SÉDUCTION

ANONYMOUS

Séduction was published in 1908. Messange, a French château in the Loire valley is the setting for this story, which chronicles the romantic and sexual development of the château's young residents. Claire de Messange, the heroine, is the object of Claude's Larcher's seduction, and to some extent, so is Claire's younger sister, Marguerite. Claude is the ward of the Marquise de Messange and admirably placed to make advances towards the two developing girls, being in the same age group and having the same status and easy intimacy, but none of the blood ties, of a sibling. But the real catalyst in terms of developing sexual sophistication is the chambermaid, Germaine. Germaine's randiness informs all aspects of this story, causing both the virginal and the more experienced to flourish and thrive in her climate of easy and abundant sexuality. But Germaine has 'a past', indeed, one so important that the author feels the need to expound upon it...

CHAPTER III:
THE STORY OF A LASCIVIOUS CHAMBERMAID

We have already mentioned that Mlle Germaine was the young girls' chambermaid. Her description: physically rather pretty, with thick hair, dark, unfathomable eyes, thin at the waist yet endowed with an ample cleavage; blithely gainsaying her twenty-five springs. All in all, with the exception of her dress, a perfect example of those crafty soubrettes which it is such a delight to ogle at the theatre through a pair of opera-glasses.

Morally speaking: an intelligent Parisian lass without the slightest scruple. Having only arrived at Messange ten months earlier, she had not managed to claim any great intimacy with the proud young girl who, as we have seen, was little disposed to encourage the familiarities of a chambermaid, even if the same was not true of little Marguerite.

The story of her life, which is pretty much the story of the Parisian underworld, is nonetheless original and merits closer attention.

Born of impoverished parents, she had spent her childhood in the streets with children the same age as herself, playing games, running wild, and commandeering as her own the ruined fortifications near where she lived, as abandoned as the weeds which grow in the cracks between the paving stones in such run-down districts. Is there anything more precocious that the children of the poor you find in Paris? Just examine such old fortifications, and you will see boys and girls playing together with the most remarkable freedom.

Young Germaine had also experienced this same life of precocious pleasures. At first, she had valiantly avoided such sexual intimacy, which she found frightening, but that had set the nerves of the other boys and girls on edge. The brunette was pretty and well-proportioned, everyone fancied her, and her natural reserve annoyed her comrades. A lad who was looked up to by the rest, because he was the strongest of the bunch, had tried to overcome her resistance, that is to say that he had made her lie on the grass and tried to lift up her skirt. But the young girl had defended herself so vigorously and shouted so loudly that the urchin had been forced to take to his heels, his curiosity unsatisfied. She had made friends with a fair-haired girl her age, who had been allowed to kiss and stroke her face. Sometimes she had even rapidly passed her hand between Germaine's legs, touching her private parts, which she longed to stroke, through the slit in her drawers. Sometimes, too, half-sitting in front of her, unfastening her own skirt and holding apart her knickers with her left hand while with the other she stroked her little hole, this friend would insert her finger in the middle and vigorously move it in and out over the little pink hillock towards the top of her sex while begging Germaine to render this service for her. While she did this, her face would become red, her breathing faster, her eyes would shine with pleasure, and her body twitch nervously at the moment of orgasm, after which she would lie back in a faint, clearly proving that the demonstration was nothing if not sincere.

Young Germaine, excited by such lascivious spectacles, would have liked deep down to experience such unknown pleasures for herself, but she was much too shy to try.

In the end, some kids, resentful and not a little inflamed by this resistance which they had never encountered before, plotted together to obtain by force that which had been refused to them until that moment. This was October time, and night had fallen more quickly than usual due to the dark clouds which filled the sky. With the pretext of playing a game, the young girl had been conducted to a deserted corner of the neighbourhood. One of the boys, who had agreed to act as look-out, gave the pre-arranged signal.

At that moment the others collectively took hold of Germaine and upended her on the grass. The girl, sensible as she was, put up a valiant fight, biting one, kicking another, begging the boys to leave her alone; but numbers were against her, and she was soon overpowered. Stretched out on her back, two of them secured her arms while two more held her feet; then, with eyes sparkling with curiosity, the boys lifted up her dress and underskirts as far as the waist; but as her pair of little white knickers prevented everyone from being able to see what they wanted to see, one of the girls who had been in the plot with the boys stepped forward, unbuttoned them and pulled them off over her boots. While keeping her skirt hitched up over her waist, her legs were forced wide apart, and everyone present, boys and girls alike, was able to satisfy their lubricious curiosity with regard to the girl's ravishing body, with its clearly delineated stomach and hips, with its thighs, firm and dimpled, separated at the junction with the lower abdomen by a charming delicate cleft like the two lips of a bright red mouth, and covered in soft light brown hair. But even this sight did not suffice for them: they turned her over in order to admire her beautiful little bottom, with its firm, well-rounded buttocks, the skin soft and white; then one of the boys parted her buttocks slightly, to the great joy of all present, and revealed her tiny crinkled rose lost at the bottom of a narrow valley. She was turned back over again, and everyone awaited their turn to caress her pink little slit and rub the crimson button, which seemed rather large for her age. Then Germaine's blonde friend, who had being dying to do this for ages, pressed through the throng of boys and, amidst their enthusiastic and ribald cries, knelt between the girl's thighs and began to lick her sexual parts avidly. Pushing back with her finger the pretty red lips, her tongue moved back and forth along the entire length of the slit, then she rolled the clitoris between her lips and flicked it rapidly with the tip of her tongue. After this game had been going on for a certain time, Germaine's stomach began to heave up and down and her thighs were racked with a nervous spasm. The crowd drew closer, fascinated by what was happening. "She's coming! She's coming! Go on, Thérèse! You can't stop now, she's about to come!" Thérèse did not need telling twice where her duty lay.

While this was going on, two boys, visibly excited, had been enjoying themselves lifting up Thérèse's skirts, who pretended not to notice; and while one of them, coiling his hand round the back of her thighs, had managed to insert one finger in the little hole between the buttocks and another into her vagina (Thérèse had lost her virginity in this way long ago) which he then rubbed briskly, the other lad, with his hand across her lower abdomen, gave her a good wanking; this time, it was Thérèse's turn to squeeze her thighs convulsively as she began to climax.

Indeed, as the lads had remarked, and in spite of the anger that this unexpected attack had caused in her, Germaine, who was by temperament a sensual brunette, though such feelings had been repressed in her until now, really did seem to have been overwhelmed by this new pleasure and was on the point of orgasm. Her face became very red and her breath became short and spasmodic; a muffled sound came from her throat, she arched her hips faster and faster, and her thighs gripped the blonde head of Thérèse as if she wanted to suffocate her. But Thérèse, who knew all the signs, recognised the onset of the final spasm, and forgot all about her own pleasure as she licked the young girl with increasing ardour, paying attention now only to her clitoris. All the teenagers, boys and girls alike, all extremely excited, now crept closer in order to watch the orgasm of their victim. Germaine, reaching the final spasm, suddenly stretched out her back as a long exclamation of pleasure came from her throat, and her fists clenched and unclenched uncontrollably; and a small jet of warm liquid squirted from the narrow slit and splashed Thérèse in the face before she had time to move it away. She herself was reaching her final voluptuous spasm and rolled heavily onto the grass.

Everybody present shouted "Bravo!", delighted with the success of their scheme; and, excited beyond control by this enticing display, they fell one upon the other in lascivious embrace, which was their usual pastime. They demonstrated their kindness to the poor girl who, ridden with shame, was hiding her face in her hands. They helped her to her feet, consoled her as best they could concerning her misadventure, and promised that they would never play such a trick on her again. Cunning young rogues that they were, they knew that Germaine's encounter with pleasure had won her over to their cause. Which, in fact, was exactly what happened. She accepted Thérèse's kisses and caresses, returned them in her turn, had all sorts of other young friends and, like them, also accommodated herself to the lubricious pleasures of boys. The latter wasted no time in deflowering her, despite her youthfulness, their fingers helping them out should their masculinity prove unequal to the task.

Later, Germaine got a job folding paper at the commercial printer's on the Rue de Rome and, like her companions, became the mistress of a typesetter.

Her lover, a tremendous expert in all the games of love, completed her education in this subject. She learned all there was to know, for he liked everything there was to like, this being the way of his natural inclinations. She found an equal pleasure in offering to her lover the marvellous grotto of love encased in its thick fleece of soft curly hair or her tiny rosette hidden in the cleft between two buttocks of an awesome beauty. Her adorable mouth, with its sensual lips, became experienced at kissing his entire body, but especially the sword of love, and procuring for him every nuance of voluptuousness. Her flexible hips lent themselves admirably to all the acrobatics of sexual passion; yet, even so, there were times when she missed the intimate caresses of girls her own age. Her lover, despite all his expertise, could not rival the infinite delicacy of her female friends whose soft caresses procured for her the supreme delights of orgasm and plunged her into an ecstasy of enchantment.

One day, as she was delivering some packets of visiting-cards to an elegant doxy on the Boulevard Haussmann (Germaine was twenty by this time), the latter found her so beguiling with her dark eyes, which set off her face admirably, that she immediately enrolled her into her service on wages that Germaine could not refuse.

Of all the schooling in sexual pleasure she had been through until that day, nothing could compare with what she learned in this fashionable house of easy morals. The day after she had entered into the service of Mme Blanche d'Antigny, her mistress rang for her. As it was not yet midday, she was still in bed. She signalled Germaine to approach.

"Come closer, my child," she said, taking her hands, "and let us talk together. How do you like being in my service?"

"Oh, very much, Madame. It is very beautiful here, and you have been so kind to me."

"You realise that being in my service means that sometimes you will have things to do which are – which are, well, rather delicate? Do you understand me? There are gentlemen, and ladies, who come to see me; if they find you pretty, it is very important that you do not displease them by being coy with them. If, from time to time, they want to kiss you, or caress you a bit, you will let them do so, it's not the end of the world. Tell me, little one, could you get used to that sort of life?"

Germaine, pretending not to understand, lowered her eyes without replying.

"Well, at least you don't say no. I think that we shall get on famously together. What I ask of you has nothing disagreeable about it, especially when one is as pretty and well-formed as you are. What's more, your complaisance in these matters will earn you all manner of little presents, which friends like to give to each other. Do you really think you could get used to it, tell me?"

"But Madame… If it's absolutely necessary… I will do my best to please you… I don't refuse…"

"That's right! Very well said! You're so nice I could eat you! In fact, come here and give me a sign of your eagerness to please me. Kiss me."

While Germaine obeyed her mistress, the latter, holding her with one arm, undid the buttons on her blouse with the other, so displaying her breasts.

"What youthfulness! How firm they are! But this is just the start. What I see here makes me curious to see the rest."

Germaine felt the hand of her mistress straying beneath her petticoats.

"Please, Madame, not that," she said, for the sake of appearances.

"What a body! Your skin is like satin! I would give a year of my life to spend a night with you as your lover. And those curly pubes of yours!"

"But, please, Madame, I don't have a lover."

"No lover! With a face as beautiful as yours, it's not possible! One should not hoard such things for one's own benefit. You are making a great mistake. If you don't like men, perhaps you like little girls of your own age, which is not so bad either."

Mme Blanche embraced Germaine again and began to play with her more intimate charms in a more determined manner than she had done until then.

"Wasn't I right when I said that you prefer the tender caresses of little girls like yourself to those of clumsy great men?"

"As you say, Madame, they are certainly more agreeable," said Germaine, who saw the direction in which her mistress was headed.

"Here's to happiness! I am sure that we will soon be great friends, unless I seem too old to you, or you find me repugnant."

"But, on the contrary, Madame is very pretty."

"A little flattery never hurt! But I wouldn't be so pretty if I didn't have full recourse to all the artifices of my toilette, whereas you, you are pretty without anything, and that is the sign of true beauty."

Even as she said this, the caresses of Germaine's mistress became more intimate.

"Please, Madame… I don't know what to say… I'm very excited…"

Mme Blanche increased her caresses, concentrating now entirely on the clitoris, which she masturbated enthusiastically.

"What big eyes you have, you little rogue. You are about to come!"

Germaine allowed herself to fall on the bed:

"Yes, Madame… Yes, Madame… I am coming… Oh, I'm com… com… com… Oh…!"

Mme Blanche, extremely excited herself as a result of this little game, jumped nimbly onto the foot of the bed, arranging

Germaine, who was so enchanted by the direction events had taken that she allowed herself to be used in this way with complete docility, in the position that suited her; then, throwing back her skirt and petticoats over her face, Mme Blanche placed her head between the delightful thighs of her pretty maid, attaching her mouth greedily to the places that her hand had a few moments before been rubbing, and began to lick, suck and bite them until Germaine gave sign that she had managed a second time to savour the supreme spasm of voluptuousness.

When the young girl had recovered from this experience, Mme Blanche asked her gently if she would care to return the same favour. Without waiting for a reply, she quickly stripped off her chemise, presenting her splendid nakedness to the enchanted eyes of her maid, lay down upon the bed, kissed Germaine, and suggested seductively in her ear that she might like to undress as well. In a trice, she too appeared in all the radiant beauty of her nakedness before her mistress, whose eyes sparkled as she enumerated without hesitation all her charms, making the beautiful girl turn around before her, as she looked on in ecstatic rapture, so that she could admire her from every angle. Then, beckoning her to the bed, she covered her in kisses and, fired with the same desire to reach orgasm in the embrace of this ravishing child, she made her kneel before her, took her head in her hands, and guided it between her thighs, to that very same place which had given Germaine so much pleasure a moment earlier. Germaine did not resist, excited and delighted in her turn at being able to rub her little muzzle in the white, sweetly perfumed flesh of her beautiful mistress. Her hands parted the thick blonde pubic mat of her mistress, and her tongue quickly found the thick button of love lodged between her lips, like a ruby in a casket of crimson velvet. Consummate as she was in such matters, she soon made her lubricious mistress, who was delighted to discover that she had taken on such a talented protégée, writhe and moan with pleasure under her exquisite caresses.

It is unnecessary to mention that this pretty duet engaged in the same activities several times more that same afternoon, and that the elegant courtesan was absolutely enchanted by her pretty, not to say extremely obliging, little maid. Nor is it necessary to enter into the details of the numerous piquant adventures that befell Germaine's lot in this highly civilised house of love. A number of friends of the house partook of this succulent dish, as they thought of her, which was truly fit for a king.

So how, you might be wondering, did someone with such a liberal education in the seductive arts manage to enter into the service of the Marquise de Messange?

Mme Blanche's lovers preferred the pretty young maid to her mistress. The latter finally took umbrage and was no longer willing to allow her maid to make up a threesome in her pleasures. Germaine, for her part, decided to give in her notice; in any event, her health was unequal to the exhausting life she was leading in Paris. She retired to her aunt's house in Touraine and sought a position, with the intention of so regaining her strength as a result of light duties in elegant surroundings, in one of the numerous châteaux which are to be found in this highly attractive part of the world. Germaine's aunt, Mme Marneffe, who was as well known at Messange as her services were appreciated, suggested her niece to the Marquise. The latter, impressed by the girl's intelligence and transparent honesty, immediately took her into her service without making further enquiry.

We shall encounter her again in the course of this story.

CHAPTER V:
THE TITILLATING ADVENTURES OF A CHAMBERMAID

We left Germaine shortly after her arrival at the Château de Messange. Her special duties consisted of looking after the two young girls: Claire and Marguerite. This château's Parisian inhabitant was delighted by her new circumstances. The superb country residence enchanted her, and the milieu in which she now found herself was like having her virginity all over again.

But such an ideal could not avoid falling victim to the lot of all roses. Her background, and above all her natural inquisitiveness, soon meant that she realised which side her bread was buttered on.

The first person to benefit from this was another servant at the château, a well-built young peasant, who quickly attracted the attention and the admiration of the young woman. Claude stumbled over them one day as he was strolling round the gardens. Hearing a noise coming from a barn used to store the hay, he was able to creep up without being seen and found himself confronted by a most arousing spectacle. Germaine and the coachman, whose name was Jean, were caught in the act, but there was nothing particularly refined about their activity, it was simply the coupling of the male and female in all its brutal savagery, and in all its magnificent power. Germaine, irresistibly attracted by the man's virility, so different from all the affectations you find in Paris, had followed Jean. Now she was defending her honour, much as she might desire him, not wishing to concede without the show of a struggle, like every girl does. But this was without reckoning on her mighty partner. Jean, excited beyond endurance by her resistance, took her in his arms and almost threw her in the hay without paying the least heed to her protestations. Ignoring the treasures of her ample cleavage, he hitched up her dress, petticoats and chemise above the waist, and prised open her legs in order to linger over the sight of her sex. Then, holding her in this position with one hand, he unbuttoned his trousers with the other and took out his enormous rod. Thick and long, red from the rush of blood and furrowed by a network of blue veins, it looked as hard as an iron bar; the head of his penis, completely uncovered by his foreskin, was more like a bludgeon. At the sight of it, Germaine became afraid.

"Jean, my love. Please, no; you won't get it in. You will hurt me! Please, Jean!"

She defended herself, clenching her thighs, pushing down her dress with both hands, trying to free herself. But Jean was by far the stronger; he had soon laid out Germaine's charming body once again, plainly exposing her sexual organs for all to see, then, placing his enormous member at the entrance of the young woman's charming little quim, he took the weight of his body on his arms and began to push, moving his backside back and forth, and breathing like a rutting beast.

Germaine, realising that all resistance was useless, resigned herself, somewhat anxiously, to her lot, for only the head of his virile member had penetrated her, and the violent shafting motions of her partner made her worry whether she was about to be torn asunder. Finally, little by little, he had fully entered her. Such is the wonderful elasticity of the side of the vagina, that her dainty grotto of love swallowed this enormous charge without the least ill effect. Germaine closed her eyes; and the sound of her breath coming by fits and starts could be heard.

Claude watched the enormous member moving back and forth. At first motionless, Germaine now began to move her thighs and the entire length of her body started to tremble. Suddenly, she arched her stomach and squeezed her fists. Her vulva, which had stretched due to all the effort it had expended, gripped her lover's rod tightly, and the resulting

contact of these two tremendous sexual organs had caused
a revolution throughout her entire being. An extraordinary
sensation, a climax such as she had never experienced before,
had completely taken possession of her; it was as if she had been
injected with fire in her veins. She cried aloud, so great was
her pleasure.

"Yes, Jean. Yes, yes! Quicker! Like that, yes! Yes! I'm coming!
I'm coming! Oh! I can feel your come inside me!"

And she gripped the body of her lover, coiling her arms
about him, squeezing him between her febrile thighs which she
crossed behind his back, as he squirted his bubbling semen
deep into her vagina while uttering exclamation of the most
utter sexual satisfaction. They remained like this, riveted one
to the other, for a long while, each savouring in silence the
voluptuous pleasure of the moment. Finally Jean, extracting
himself from the passionate embrace of his ravishing and
radiant mistress, slowly withdrew his member from the body
of the beautiful young woman, and the white liquid of love
dribbled from her crimson vulva across her buttocks in elegant
testimony of the copious nature of his ejaculation: Germaine's
thighs were completely inundated.

This scene, as violent as it was unexpected, had utterly
overwhelmed Claude. His blood was boiling in his veins, an
irresistible ardour had seized hold of him, even as he had
watched events unfurl, and his hands had automatically
clutched at his rod which had become swollen and enormous
notwithstanding the fact that it was impeded by his trousers.
He had unbuttoned his flies and, taking his burning erection
in one hand, assisted matters in the natural manner such that,
at the very same time as Germaine and her partner, he too had
experienced the same spasm which had left him inundated with
the same hot liquid.

For the next few days the young man could think of nothing
else but what he had witnessed, he even dreamed about it.

A strong urge took hold of him to possess the young woman physically himself.

He resisted the impulse however, not wishing to profane the love he harboured for Claire, realising the extent of his betrayal towards his charming friend should he become the lover of a woman employed in her service. But how can one resist a desire so intense that it follows you everywhere like a shadow without giving you a moment's peace? "After all, love has nothing to do with it," he said to himself, "it's just an animal instinct that will go away again as soon as it has been satisfied!"

Unable to bear it a moment longer, one evening he made his way to Germaine's bedroom just at the moment that she was preparing for bed and was half-undressed; in fact, all she had on was her chemise, and even that had slipped from her shoulders to reveal the young woman's firm pink breasts which stood up proudly. He remained in the doorway for a moment unable to make up his mind, seized at the same time with admiration for the girl's almost naked body and trepidation at his audacious conduct. Germaine quickly backed away from him, red with surprise; she reached for her clothes, but Claude did not give her time to put anything on. Casting aside his earlier hesitation, he closed and bolted the door behind him and threw himself on the young girl, sweeping her into his arms, and kissing her on the mouth, the neck, and on her ravishing breasts, having prised away Germaine's arms with which she sought to protect herself, while his lascivious hand lost itself between Germaine's thighs, fondling the young woman's most intimate charms beneath the thin cloth of her chemise, feeling the rustle of her pubic hair and the soft, warm sensation of her sexual parts under his fingers.

Germaine, taken by surprise by this unexpected attack, only defended herself feebly, more for the sake of form than anything else, because she was in reality overjoyed by such an adventure. She found Claude very attractive, and she had already considered trying to seduce him. Thus, even while feeling herself the prey of this handsome youth, whose ardent kisses reigned down on her mouth, her breasts became erect, her entire being quivered under his passionate caresses, and a powerful urge to possess him seized hold of her. She utterly abandoned herself to Claude who, realising she was his, guided her to the bed and lay down next to her but upside down. He raised her chemise and, fascinated by her naked body, applied his mouth to the part that his hand had just been exciting. He kissed Germaine greedily, taking her vulva in his mouth and sucking her clitoris, which was already hard, while she for her part bucked up and down under his luxurious embrace, squeezing the young man's head between her thighs.

After a moment, Claude pulled his head away, rolled over on his back, and pulled Germaine's body on top of him in such a manner that his head remained between the beautiful girl's thighs. He slipped his hands beneath her buttocks and redoubled the passionate stroking motions he was making along the entire length of her clitoris. Meanwhile the sexual odour of her vulva made him almost drunk with excitement as he forced his tongue into the warm depths of her vagina, and he breathed in the smell of the moist juices which emanated from her sexual parts, stimulated by all the rubbing they had received.

Germaine, in the grip of pleasure, was panting and writhing about uncontrollably on the bed. Her head was turned in the direction of Claude's feet; she unbuttoned his breeches and took out his gorgeous member, hot and swollen with desire. First she stroked it, then she placed it in her mouth, sucking it passionately, in this way repaying Claude for the kisses she had received. But Claude was too excited to restrain himself and would have come almost immediately had he not moderated Germaine's enthusiasm.

"Wait," he cried, "not so fast. That way we can both come at the same time."

Thrusting his head once again between the thighs of the beautiful girl, he redoubled his caresses, letting his tongue wander all over her lower abdomen and buttocks, exploring every crevice and licking the little wrinkled pink hole, whose elasticity he tested by inserting his entire finger. This he did so easily that he proved that this charming place was no stranger to Cupid's virile member.

In the throes of such lascivious caresses and mutual excitement, the young couple uttered a stream of pleasurable exclamations. Claude began once again to lick the engorged clitoris of the young woman as he seized hold of her swollen breasts with their erect nipples. One could tell that Germaine was approaching the supreme pleasure from the manner in which her sexual organs began to swell, the febrile nature of her movements, the almost frantic manner in which she clasped her partner, and the energetic manner in which she masturbated Claude while taking his entire rod in her mouth.

Suddenly she let out a gasp and entirely stopped what she was doing. At the same time Claude felt his face grow wet. Rather than withdrawing though, he squeezed the fragrant vulva between his lips and swallowed the milky fluid which was squirting out. He himself had arrived at the pinnacle of pleasure and, feeling his lover's sexual spasm, he lost control of himself and filled his lover's mouth with his burning sperm. Germaine, who loved the white liquid of love, was careful not to open her lips; squeezing his rod with her hand to choke off the release of the sperm, she allowed it to escape only a little at a time, so prolonging her friend's pleasure, swallowing it drop by drop, so as not to waste the least particle.

It would be superfluous to remark how delighted our two lovers were by their adventure and the intoxicating nature of the voluptuous sensations they experienced in each other's arms. Germaine, elated at possessing a lover who was so gentle with her, covered him in kisses and the tenderest caresses. She undressed Claude so that he was quite naked and she could study his splendid, svelte body. For his part, Claude removed Germaine's chemise so that he could admire her beauty at his leisure, especially her remarkable dark fleece, thick and curly, which complemented the velvety whiteness of her skin. Her resplendent blonde hair, which reached down to her waist, the lustre of her beautiful brown eyes, the sparkle of her teeth, and the heightened colour which every woman has just after making love – all these exquisite features offered to Claude's lingering gaze excited him to such a point that his virility, temporarily blunted by the sweet agony of pleasure he had just experienced under the prolonged oral stimulation of his friend, was quickly rekindled.

The young woman, delighted by this rapid renaissance, which is the sincerest compliment that a man can pay to a woman's charms, offered herself to her lover again, without restriction, so that he had the choice between her ravishing mound of Venus or the narrow retreat hidden between her firm young buttocks. Claude's first preference was to explore this little hole because this was something new to him. Germaine explained to him what he should do and, turning round, knelt before him, her body bent forwards, her head buried in a pillow, parting her thighs for him and revealing the prettiest little arsehole imaginable. Claude, kneeling behind her, admired her splendid buttocks as he caressed them. He placed a globule of his saliva on the tiny orifice and, in order to facilitate penetration, another on the end of his swollen prick, then, parting her buttocks a little further with his hands, he placed his member against her narrow entrance, pushed gently forwards, and saw the full length of his rod slide slowly into her dilating anus until it disappeared. Germaine moved her backside back and forth gently and skilfully so that it was not long before Claude's member, gripped by her arse as if in a vice, ejaculated once again, squirting a fresh inundation of milky fluid into his lover's bowels, the constriction of the anus preventing him from draining himself in a single movement. At the same time the young man experienced the most exquisite sense of bliss which Germaine, as Claude had also been fondling her clitoris with his hand, entirely shared.

Claude generously thanked his friend for so kindly obliging him in this way. It was not until much later that he regained his own bedroom, and only after he had made the young woman climax yet again. This time, he had her in the same manner as Jean, the coachman, and his rod, thrust deep into Germaine's vagina, left a final and copious libation there. Lying on top of the naked body of his pretty mistress, mouth to mouth, tightly enlaced, they experienced once more the supreme delights of love-making.

Claude, who had grown rather fond of these charming games, wanted to repeat them as often as he could. He disported himself with the pretty maid, teasing her at all times of the day, tried to make love at the most inopportune moments in whichever room he accidentally stumbled across her, and even played one or two tricks on her of a rather mean nature.

Thus it was, one day, that finding Germaine leaning from a first floor window, talking with Claire and her sister, who were both in the garden, the absurd idea possessed him to have his way with her right then and there. Before she had time to realise what was going on, he had lowered the sash-window over the small of her back and closed the blinds. Then, hitching up her petticoats, and taking full advantage of the fact that she was completely trapped, he thrust his member into her vagina from behind at the same time as, slipping one of his hands round her front, he began to stroke and rub her clitoris. Despite her initial discontent, both on account of the inopportune nature of the attack and the fact that she was being taken from the rear, Germaine soon began to enjoy herself, wiggling her backside in the most provocative fashion; and Claude clearly heard the tinkling laughter of the two young girls outside, amazed at their maid's sudden stammer, her redness, how white her eyes had become, and the apparent loss of control she was suffering of her facial muscles while, unbeknown to them, she had an orgasm.

The innocent little dears did not for a single instant guess the real cause of Germaine's confusion, which they found so amusing, imagining that it was the consequence of a nervous reflex provoked by the fall of the window.

GALLERY IV

THE WAY OF A MAN WITH A MAID

ANONYMOUS

There is no date available for The Way of a Man with a Maid although events described place it firmly towards the end of the Edwardian era. Both hansoms and 'taxis' are mentioned, which would date the action after 1903, when the first internal combustion cab appeared, but when there were still 11,000 horse-drawn cabs in London. Fanny, the maid, is the servant of Alice, who is, confusingly, the 'Maid' of the book's title. The 'Man' is played by Jack, the caddish hero determined to have his revenge upon society girl Alice for having jilted him, in his words, 'cruelly and unjustifiably'. Not satisfied with the imprisonment, bondage, mild torture by means of tickling, double defloration and thorough ravishment of Alice (who adores every second of it), the dastardly Jack persuades her to bring Fanny along for similar treatment in the specially designed, soundproof room he calls 'The Snuggery'. This time, however, Alice wants to have a hand in the 'torture', as her maid can be 'a pert minx at times' and spanking her bottom would 'do her a lot of good'. Jack and Alice hatch a plot to tame Fanny between them. Fanny proves a delightful and delighted victim…

Next afternoon, after seeing that everything was in working order in the Snuggery, I threw open both doors as if carelessly, and, taking off my coat as if not expecting any visitors, I proceeded to potter about the room, keeping a vigilant eye on the stairs. Before long I heard footsteps on the landing, but pretended not to know that any one was there till Alice tapped merrily on the door saying, 'May we come in, Jack?'

'Good heavens, Alice!' I exclaimed in pretended surprise as I struggled hurriedly to get into my coat. 'Come in! How do you do? Where have you dropped from?'

'We've been shopping. This is my maid, Jack.' (I bowed and smiled, receiving in return from Fanny a distinctly pert and not too respectful nod.) 'As we were close by, I thought I would take the chance of finding you in and take away that enlargement if it is ready.'

By this time I had struggled into my coat. 'It's quite ready,' I replied. 'I'll go and get it, and I don't know why those doors should stand so unblushingly open,' I added with a laugh.

Having closed them, noiselessly locking them, I disappeared into the alcove I used for myself, and pretended to search for the enlargement, my real object being to give Alice a chance of letting Fanny know the nature of the room. Instinctively she divined my idea, and I heard her say, 'This is the room I was telling you about, Fanny. Look at the double doors, the padded walls, the rings, the pillars, the hanging pulley straps! Isn't it queer?'

Fanny looked about her with evident interest. 'It is a funny room, Miss! And what are those little places for?' pointing to the two alcoves.

'We do not know, Fanny,' Alice replied. 'Mr Jack uses them for his photographic work now.'

As she spoke, I emerged with a large print which was to represent the supposed enlargement, and gave it to Alice who at once proceeded to closely examine it.

I saw that Fanny's eyes were wandering all over the room, and I moved over to her. 'A strange room, Fanny, eh?' I remarked. 'Is it not still? No sound from outside can get in, and no noise from inside can get out! That's a fact; we've tested it thoroughly.'

'Lor', Mr Jack!' she replied in her forward familiar way, turning her eyes on me in a most audacious and bold way, then resuming her survey of the room.

While she was doing so, I hastily inspected her. She was a distinctly pretty girl, tall, slenderly but strongly built, with an exquisitely well-developed figure. A slightly turned-up nose and dark flashing eyes gave her face a saucy look which her free style of moving accentuated, while her dark hair and rich colouring indicated a warm-blooded and passionate temperament. I easily could understand that Alice with her gentle ways was no match for Fanny; and I fancied that I should have my work cut out for me before I got her arms fastened to the pulley ropes.

Alice now moved towards us, print in hand. 'Thanks awfully, Jack, it's lovely!' And she began to roll it up. 'Now Fanny, we must be off!'

'Don't bother about the print, I'll send it after you,' I said. 'And where are you off to now?'

'Nowhere in particular,' she replied. 'We'll look at the shops and the people. Goodbye Jack!'

'One moment!' I interposed. 'You were talking the other day about some perfection of a lady's maid whom you didn't want to lose, (Fanny smiled complacently) 'but whose tantrums and ill tempers were getting more than you could stand.' (Fanny here began to look angry.) 'Somebody suggested that you should give her a good spanking,' (Fanny assumed a contemptuous air) 'or, if you couldn't manage it yourself, you should get some one to do it for you.' (Fanny here glared at me.) 'Is this the young lady?'

Alice nodded, with a curious glance at Fanny, who was now evidently getting into one of her passions.

'Well, as you've nothing to do this afternoon and she happens to be here, and this room is so eminently suitable for the purpose, shall I take the young woman in hand for you and teach her a lesson?'

Before Alice could reply, Fanny with a startled exclamation darted to the door, evidently bent on escape, but in spite of her vigorous twists of the handle and shakings the door refused to open, for the simple reason that unnoticed by her I had locked it. Instantly divining that she was a prisoner, she turned hurriedly round to watch our movements, but she was too late!

With a quickness learnt on the football field, I was on to her and pinned her arms to her sides in a grip that she could not break out of despite her frantic struggles. 'Let me go...let me go, Mr Jack!' she screamed. I simply chuckled as I knew I had her safe now. I had to exert all my strength and skill, for she was extraordinarily strong and her furious rage added to her power, but, in spite of her desperate resistance, I forced her to the hanging pulleys where Alice was eagerly waiting for us. With astonishing quickness she made fast the ropes to Fanny's wrists and set the machinery going, and in a few seconds the surprised girl found herself standing erect with her arms dragged up taut over her head.

'Well done, Jack!' exclaimed Alice as she delightedly surveyed the still struggling Fanny. The latter was indeed a lovely subject of contemplation, as, with heaving bosom, flushed cheeks, and eyes that sparkled with rage, she stood panting, endeavouring to get back her breath, while her agitated fingers vainly strove to get her wrists free from the pulley ropes. We watched her in victorious silence, waiting for the outburst of wrathful fury which we felt would come as soon as she was able to speak.

It soon came! 'How dare you, Mr Jack!' Fanny burst out as she flashed her great piercing eyes at us, her whole body trembling with anger. 'How dare you treat me like this! Let me go at once, or as sure as I am alive I'll have the law on you and also on that mealy-mouthed smooth-faced demure hypocrite that calls herself my mistress indeed! Who looks on while a poor girl is vilely treated and won't raise a finger to help her! Let me go at once, Mr Jack and I'll promise to say and do nothing. But my God,' (here her voice became shrill with overpowering rage) 'my God if you don't, I'll make it hot for the pair of you when I get out!' And she glared at us in her impotent fury.

'Your mistress has asked me to give you a lesson, Fanny,' I replied calmly, 'and I'm going to do so. The sooner you recognise how helpless you really are, and will submit yourself to us, the sooner it will be over; but if you are foolish enough to resist, you'll have a long doing and a bad time! Now, if I let you loose, will you take your clothes off quietly?'

'My God, no!' she cried indignantly, but in spite of herself she blushed vividly.

'Then we'll take them off for you!' was my cool reply. 'Come along, Alice, you understand girl's clothes, you undo them and I'll get them off somehow.'

Quickly Alice sprang up, trembling with excitement, and together we approached Fanny, who shrieked defiance and threats at us in her impotent fury as she struggled desperately to get free. But as soon as she felt Alice's fingers unfastening her garments, her rage changed to horrible apprehension; and as one by one they slipped off her, she began to realise how helpless she was. 'Don't Miss!' she ejaculated pitifully. 'My God! Stop her, Sir!' she pleaded, the use of these more respectful terms of address sufficiently proclaiming her changed attitude. But we were obdurate, and soon Fanny stood with only her chemise and under-vest left on her, her shoes and stockings having been dragged off her at the special request of Alice, whose unconcealed enjoyment of the work of stripping her maid was delicious to witness.

She now took command of operations. Pointing to a chair just in front of Fanny she exclaimed, 'Sit there, Jack, and watch Fanny as I take off her last garments!'

'For God's sake, Miss, don't strip me naked!' shrieked Fanny who seemed to expect that she would be left in her chemise and to whom the sudden intimation that she was to be exposed naked came with an appalling shock. 'Oh Sir, for God's sake, stop her!' she cried appealing to me as she saw me take my seat right in front of her and felt Alice's fingers begin to undo the shoulder-strap fastenings which alone kept her scanty garments on her. 'Miss Alice...Miss Alice! Don't...for God's sake, don't!' she screamed in a fresh outburst of dismay as she felt her vest slip down her body to her feet and she knew her only covering was about to follow. In despair she tugged frantically at the ropes which made her arms so absolutely helpless, her agitated quivering fingers betraying her mental agony.

'Steady, Fanny, steady!' exclaimed Alice to her struggling maid as she proceeded to unfasten the chemise, her eyes gleaming with lustful cruelty: 'Now, Jack!' she said warningly, then let go, stepping back a pace herself the better to observe the effect. Down swept the chemise, and Fanny stood stark naked!

'Oh! Oh!' she wailed, crimson with shame, her face hidden on her bosom which now was wildly heaving in agitation. It was a wonderful spectacle! In the foreground was Fanny, naked, helpless, in an agony of shame, in the background but close to her was Alice exquisitely costumed and hatted, gloating over the sight of her maid's absolute nudity, her eyes intently fixed on the gloriously luscious curves of Fanny's hips, haunches and bottom.

I managed to catch her eye and motioned to her to come and sit on my knees that we might, in each other's close company, study her maid's naked charms so reluctantly being exhibited to us. With one long last look she obeyed my summons. As she seated herself on my knees she threw her arms round my neck and kissed me rapturously whispering, 'Jack, isn't she delicious!'

I nodded smilingly, then in turn murmured in her ear, 'And how do you like the game, dear?'

Alice blushed divinely; a strange languishing voluptuous half-wanton half-cruel look came into her eyes. Placing her lips carefully on mine she gave me three long-drawn kisses, the significance of which I could not possibly misunderstand, then whispered almost hoarsely, 'Jack, let me do all the...torturing and be content this time, with...fucking Fanny...and me too, darling!'

'She's your maid and, so to speak, your property, dear,' I replied softly, 'so arrange matters just as you like; I'll leave it all to you and won't interfere unless you want me to do anything'.

She kissed me gratefully, then turned her eyes on Fanny, who during this whispered colloquy had been standing trembling, her face still hidden from us, her legs pressed closely against each other as if to shield as much as possible her cunt from our sight.

I saw Alice's eyes wander over Fanny's naked body with evident pleasure, dwelling first on her magnificent lines and curves, then on her lovely breasts, and finally on the mass of dark curling moss-like hair that covered her cunt. She was a most deliciously voluptuous girl, one calculated to excite Alice to the utmost pitch of lust of which she was capable, and, while secretly regretting that my share in the process of taming Fanny was to be somewhat restricted, I felt that I would enjoy the rare opportunity of seeing how a girl, hitherto chaste and well-regulated, would yield to her sexual instincts and passions when she had placed at her absolute disposal one of her own sex in a state of absolute nakedness.

Presently Alice whispered to me, 'Jack, I'm going to feel her!' I smiled and nodded.

Fanny must have heard her, for as Alice rose she for the first time raised her head and cried, 'No, Miss, please Miss, don't touch me!' and again she vainly strained at her fastenings, her face quivering and flushed with shame. But disregarding her maid's piteous entreaties, Alice passed behind her, then kneeling down began to stroke Fanny's bottom, a hand to each cheek.

'Don't Miss!' yelled Fanny, arching herself outwards and away from Alice, and thereby unconsciously throwing the region of her cunt into greater prominence. But with a smile of cruel gratification, Alice continued her sweet occupation, sometimes squeezing, sometimes pinching Fanny's glorious half moons, now and then extending her excursions over Fanny's round plump thighs, once indeed letting her hands creep up them till I really thought (and so did Fanny from the way she screamed and wriggled) that she was about to feel Fanny's cunt.

Suddenly Alice rose, rushed to me, and kissing me ardently whispered excitedly, 'Oh Jack, she's just lovely! Such flesh, such a skin! I've never felt a girl before, I've never touched any girl's breasts or...cunt...except of course my own,' she added archly: 'and I'm wild at the idea of handling Fanny! Watch me carefully, darling, and if I don't do it properly, tell me!' And back to Fanny she rushed, evidently in a state of intense excitement.

This time Alice didn't kneel, but placed herself close behind Fanny, her dress in fact touching her. Then suddenly she threw her arms round Fanny's body and seized her breasts. 'Miss Alice, don't!' shrieked Fanny, struggling desperately, her flushed face betraying her agitation.

'Oh how lovely...how delicious...how sweet!' cried Alice, wild with delight and sexual excitement as she squeezed and played with Fanny's voluptuous breasts. Her head with its exquisite hat was just visible over Fanny's right shoulder, while her dainty dress showed on each side of the struggling, agitated girl, throwing into bold relief her glorious shape and accentuating in the most piquant way Fanny's stark nakedness. Entranced I gazed at the voluptuous spectacle, my prick struggling to break through the fly of my trousers. Fanny had now ceased her cries and was enduring in silence, broken only by her involuntary 'ohs' caused by the violation of her breasts by Alice, whose little hands could scarcely grasp the luscious morsels of Fanny's flesh they were so subtlely torturing, but which nevertheless succeeded in squeezing and compressing them and generally playing with them till the poor girl gasped in her shame and agony: 'Oh, Miss Alice...Miss Alice...stop...stop!' her head falling forward in her extreme agitation.

With a smile of intense satisfaction, Alice suspended her torturing operations and gently stroked and soothed Fanny's breasts till the more regular breathing of the latter indicated that she had in a great degree regained her self-control. Then her expression changed. A cruel hungry light came into her eyes as she smiled wickedly and meaningfully at me then I saw her hands quit Fanny's breasts and glide over her stomach till they arrived at Fanny's cunt.

Fanny shrieked as if she had been stung. 'Miss Alice...Miss Alice...don't...don't touch me there!...Oh...oh my God! Miss Alice...oh Miss Alice! Take your hands away!' at the same time twisting and writhing in a perfectly wonderful way in her frantic endeavours to escape from her mistress's hands, the fingers of which were now hidden in her cunt's mossy covering as they inquisitively travelled all over her Mount Venus and along the lips of the orifice itself. For some little time they contented themselves with feeling and pressing and toying caressingly with Fanny's cunt, then I saw one hand pause while the first finger of the other gently began to work its way between the pink lips and disappear into the sweet cleft. 'Don't Miss!' yelled Fanny, her agonised face now scarlet while in her distress she desperately endeavoured to defend her cunt by throwing her legs in turn across her groin, to Alice's delight, whose face betrayed the intense pleasure she was tasting in thus making her maid undergo such subtle torture.

Presently I noted an unmistakable look of surprise in her eyes. Her lips parted as if in astonishment, while her hand seemed to redouble its attack on Fanny's cunt, then she exclaimed, 'Why Fanny! What's this?'

'Oh don't tell Mr Jack, Miss!' shrieked Fanny, letting her legs drop as she could no longer endure the whole weight of her struggling body on her slender wrists. 'Don't let him know!'

My curiosity was naturally aroused and intently I watched the movements of Alice's hand which the fall of Fanny's legs brought again into full view. Her forefinger was buried up to the knuckle in her maid's cunt! The mystery was explained. Fanny was not a virgin!

Alice seemed staggered by her discovery. Abruptly she quitted Fanny, rushed to me, threw herself on my knees, then flinging her arms round my neck she whispered excitedly in my ear, 'Jack, she's been...had by someone...my finger went right in!'

'So I noticed, darling!' I replied quietly as I kissed her flushed cheek. 'Its rather a pity! But she'll stand more fucking than if she was a virgin, and you must arrange your programme accordingly. I think you'd better let her rest a bit now, her arms will be getting numb from being kept her over head; let's fasten her to that pillar by passing her arms round it and shackling her wrists together. She can then rest a bit; and while she is recovering from her struggles hadn't you better...slip your clothes off also, for your eyes hint that you will want...something before long!'

Alice blushed prettily, then whispered as she kissed me ardently, 'I'd like...something now, darling!' Then she ran away to her dressing room.

Left alone with Fanny, I proceeded to transfer her from the pulleys to the pillar. It was not a difficult task, as her arms were too numb to be of much use to her and she seemed stupefied at our discovery that her maidenhead no longer existed. Soon I had her firmly fastened with her back pressing against the pillar. This new position had two great advantages: she could no longer hide her face from us and the backwards pull of her arms threw her breasts out. She glanced timidly at me as I stood admiring her luscious nakedness, waiting for Alice's return.

'When did this little slip happen, Fanny?' I asked quietly.

She coloured vividly. 'When I was seventeen, Sir,' she replied softly but brokenly. 'I was drugged...and didn't know till after it was done! It's never been done again, Mr Jack,' she continued with pathetic earnestness in her voice, 'never! I swear it, Sir!' Then after a short pause she whispered, 'Oh Mr Jack! Let me go!...I'll come to you whenever you wish...and let you do what you like...but...I'm afraid of Miss Alice today...she seems so strange!...Oh my God! She's naked!' she screamed in genuine alarm as Alice came out of her toilet room with only her shoes and stockings on, and her large matinee hat, a most coquettishly piquantly indecent object! Poor Fanny went red at the sight of her mistress and didn't know where to look as Alice came dancing along, her eyes noting with evident approval the position into which I had placed her maid.

'*Mes compliments, mademoiselle!*' I said with a low bow as she came up.

She smiled and blushed, but was too intent on Fanny to joke with me. 'That's lovely, Jack!' she exclaimed after a careful inspection of her now trembling maid. 'But surely she can get loose?'

'Oh no!' I replied with a smile. 'But if you like I'll fasten her ankles together.'

'No, no, Sir!' cried Fanny.

' Yes, Jack, do!' exclaimed Alice, her eyes gleaming with lust and delight. She evidently had thought out some fresh torture for Fanny, and with the closest attention, she watched me as I linked her maid's slender ankles together in spite of the poor girl's entreaties.

'I like that much better, Jack,' said Alice, smiling her thanks. Then catching me by the elbow, she pushed me towards my alcove saying, 'We both will want you presently, Jack,' looking roguishly at me, 'so get ready! But tell me first, where are the feathers?'

'Oh that's your game!' I replied with a laugh. She nodded, colouring slightly, and I told her where she would find them. I had a peep-hole in my alcove through which I could see all that passed in the room, and, being curious to watch the two girls, I placed myself by it as I slowly undressed myself.

Having found the feathers, Alice placed the box near her, then going right up to Fanny she took hold of her own breasts with her hands, raised them till they were level with Fanny's, then, leaning on Fanny so that their stomachs were in close contact, she directed her breasts against Fanny's, gently rubbing her nipples against Fanny's while she looked intently into Fanny's eyes. It was a most curious sight! The girls' naked bodies were touching from their ankles to their breasts, their cunts were so close to each other that their hairs formed one mass, while their faces were so near to each other that the brim of Alice's matinee hat projected over Fanny's forehead.

Not a word was said. For about half a minute Alice continued to rub her breasts gently against Fanny's with her eyes fixed on Fanny's downcast face, then suddenly I saw both naked bodies quiver, and then Fanny raised her head and for the first time responded to Alice's glance, her colour coming and going. At the same moment, a languorous voluptuous smile swept over Alice's face, and gently she kissed Fanny, who flushed rosy red but as far as I could see did not respond.

'Won't you...love me, Fanny?' I heard Alice say softly but with a curious strained voice. Immediately I understood the position. Alice was lusting after Fanny! I was delighted. It was clear that Fanny had not yet reciprocated Alice's passion, and I determined that Alice should have every opportunity of satisfying her lust on Fanny's naked helpless body, till the latter was converted to tribadism with Alice as the object.

'Won't you...love me, Fanny?' again asked Alice softly, now supplementing the play of her breasts against Fanny's by insinuating and significant pressings of her stomach against Fanny's, again kissing the latter sweetly. But Fanny made no response, and Alice's eyes grew hard with a steely cruel glitter which boded badly for Fanny.

Quitting Fanny, Alice went straight to the box of feathers, picked one out, and returned to Fanny, feather in hand. The sight of her moving about thus, her breasts dancing, her hips swaying, her cunt and bottom in full view, her nakedness intensified by her piquant costume of hat, shoes and stockings, was enough to galvanise a corpse; it set my blood boiling with lust and I could hardly refrain from rushing out and compelling her to let me quench my fires in her. I did however resist the temptation, and rapidly undressed to my shoes and socks so as to be ready to take advantage of any chance that either of the girls might offer. I remained in my alcove with my eye to the peephole as I was curious to witness the denouement of this strangely voluptuous scene, which Alice evidently wished to play single handed.

No sooner did Fanny catch sight of the feather than she screamed, 'No...no Miss Alice...don't tickle me!' at the same time striving frantically to break the straps that linked together her wrists and her ankles. But my tackle was too strong. Alice meanwhile had caught up a cushion, which she placed at Fanny's feet, right in front of her. She knelt on it, rested her luscious bottom on her heels, and, having settled herself down comfortably, Alice, with a smile in which cruelty and malice were strangely blended, gloatingly contemplated for a moment her maid's naked and agitated body, then slowly and deliberately applied the tip of the feather to Fanny's cunt.

'Oh my God! Miss Alice, don't!' yelled Fanny, writhing in delicious contortions in her desperate endeavours to dodge the feather. 'Don't Miss!' she shrieked, as Alice, keenly enjoying her maid's distress and her vain efforts to avoid the torture, proceeded delightedly to pass the feather lightly along the sensitive lips of Fanny's cunt and finally set to work to tickle Fanny's clitoris, thereby sending her so nearly into hysterical convulsions that I felt it time I interposed.

As I emerged from my alcove Alice caught sight of me and dropped her hand as she turned towards me, her eyes sparkling with lascivious delight! 'Oh Jack! Did you see her?' she cried excitedly.

'I heard her, dear,' I replied ambiguously, 'and began to wonder whether you were killing her, so came I out to see.'

'Not a bit of it!' she cried, hugely pleased. 'I'm going to give her another turn!' – a declaration that produced from Fanny the most pitiful pleadings, which seemed only to increase Alice's cruel satisfaction, and she was proceeding to be as good as her word when I stopped her.

'You'd better let me first soothe her irritated senses, dear,' I said, and with one hand I caressed and played with Fanny's full and voluptuous breasts, which I found tense and firm under her sexual excitement, while with the other I stroked and felt her cunt, a procedure that evidently afforded her considerable relief although, at another time, it doubtless would have provoked shrieks and cries. She had not spent, though she must have been very close to doing it. I saw that I must watch Alice very closely indeed during the turn she was going to give Fanny for my special delectation, lest the catastrophe I was so desirous of avoiding should occur, for in my mind I had decided that, when Alice had finished tickling Fanny, she should have an opportunity of satisfying her lustful cravings for her maid.

While feeling Fanny's cunt, I naturally took the opportunity to see if Alice's penetrating finger had met with any difficulty entering and had thus caused Fanny the pain that her shrieks and wriggles had indicated. I found the way in intensely tight, a confirmation of her story and statement that nothing had gone in since the rape was committed on her. Although therefore I could not have the gratification of taking her virginity, I felt positive that I should have a delicious time and that, practically, I should be violating her, and I wondered into which of the two delicious cunts now present I would shoot my surging and boiling discharge as I dissolved in love's sweetest ecstasies.

'Now, Alice, I think she is ready for you,' I said when I had stroked and felt Fanny to my complete satisfaction.

'No, no, Miss Alice,' shrieked Fanny in frantic terror, 'For God's sake don't tickle me again!'

Disregarding her cries, Alice, who had with difficulty restrained her impatience, quickly again applied the feather to Fanny's cunt, and a wonderful spectacle followed! Fanny's shrieks, cries and entreaties filled the room as she wriggled and squirmed and twisted herself about in the most bewitchingly provocative manner, while Alice, with parted lips and eyes that simply glistened with lust, remorselessly tickled her maid's cunt with every refinement of cruelty, fresh shriek and convulsion bringing a delighted look onto her face. Motionless I watched the pair, till I noticed Fanny's breasts stiffen and become tense. Immediately I covered her cunt with my hand, saying to Alice, 'Stop, dear! She's had as much as she can stand.' Then reluctantly she desisted from her absorbing occupation and rose, her naked body quivering with aroused but unsatisfied lust.

Now was the time for me to try and effect what I had in mind, viz. the introduction of both girls to tribadism. 'Let us move Fanny to the large couch and fasten her down before she recovers herself,' I hastily whispered to Alice. Quickly we set her loose. Between us we carried her, half-fainting, to the large settee couch where we lay her on her back and made fast her wrists to the two top corners and her ankles to the two lower ones. We now had only to set the machinery going and she would lie in the position I desired, namely spread-eagled.

Alice now clutched me excitedly and whispered hurriedly, 'Jack, do me before she comes to herself and before she can see us. I'm just mad for it!' And indeed with her flushed cheeks, humid eyes, and heaving breasts this was very evident.

But although I also was bursting with lust, and eager to fuck either Alice or her maid, it would not have suited my programme to do so. I wanted Alice to fuck Fanny. I wanted the first spending of both girls to be mutually provoked by the friction of their excited cunts, one against the other. This was why I stopped Alice from tickling her maid into spending, and it was for this reason that I had extended Fanny on her back in such a position that her cunt should be at Alice's disposal.

'Hold on, darling, for a bit,' I whispered back; 'you'll soon see why! I want it as badly as you do, my sweet, but am fighting against it till the proper time comes. Run away now and take off your hat, for it will now be only in the way. And I smiled significantly as I kissed her. Alice promptly obeyed. I then seated

myself on the couch by the side of Fanny, who was still lying
with eyes closed, but breathing almost normally, and bending
over her I closely inspected her cunt to ascertain whether
she had or had not spent under the terrific tickling it had just
received. I could find no traces whatever, but to make sure
I gently drew the lips apart and peered into the sweet coral
cleft, but again saw no traces. The touch of my fingers on her
cunt however had roused Fanny from her semi-stupor and she
dreamily opened her eyes, murmuring, 'Oh Sir, don't!' as she
recognised that I was her assailant, then she looked hurriedly
round as in if search of Alice.

'Your mistress will be here immediately,' I said with a smile.
'She has only gone away to take off her hat.' The look of terror
returned to her eyes, and she exclaimed, 'Oh Mr Jack, do let me
go, she'll kill me!'

'Oh no!' I replied as I laughed at her agitation. 'Oh no, Fanny,
on the contrary! She's now going to do to you the sweetest, nicest
and kindest thing one girl can do to another. Here she comes.'

I rose as Alice came up full of pleasurable excitement as to
what was now going to happen, and I slipped my arm lovingly
round her waist. She looked eagerly at her now trembling maid,
then whispered, 'Is she ready for us again, Jack?'

'Yes, dear,' I answered softly. 'While you were away taking off
your hat, I thought it as well to see in what condition her cunt
was after its tickling. I find it very much irritated and badly in
want of Nature's soothing essence. You, darling, are also much
in the same state, your cunt also wants soothing. So I want you
girls to soothe each other. Get on to Fanny, dear, take her in your
arms. Arrange yourself on her so that your cunt lies on hers. and
then gently rub yours against it. Soon both of you will be tasting
the sweetest ecstasy. In other words, fuck Fanny, dear!'

Alice looked at me in wondering admiration. As she
began to comprehend my suggestion, her face broke into
delighted smiles, and when I stooped to kiss her she exclaimed

rapturously, 'Oh Jack, how sweet...how delicious!' as she gazed eagerly at Fanny.

But the latter seemed horrified at the idea of being submitted thus to her mistress's lustful passion and embraces, and attempted to escape, crying in her dismay, 'No, no, Sir! Oh no, Miss! I don't want it, please!'

'But I do, Fanny!' cried Alice with sparkling eyes as she gently but firmly pushed her struggling maid on to her back and held her down forcibly, till I had pulled all four straps tight, so that Fanny lay flat with her arms and legs wide apart in Maltese-Cross fashion. A simply entrancing spectacle! Then slipping my hands under her buttocks, I raised her middle till Alice was able to push a hard cushion under her bottom, the effect of which was to make her cunt stand out prominently. Then turning to Alice, who had assisted in these preparations with the keenest interest but evident impatience, I said, 'Now, dear, there she is! Set to work and violate your maid.'

In a flash Alice was on the couch and on her knees between Fanny's widely parted legs. Excitedly she threw herself on her maid, passed her arms round her and hugged her closely, as she showered kisses on Fanny's still protesting mouth till the girl had to stop for breath. With a few rapid movements she arranged herself on her maid so that the two luscious pairs of breasts were pressing against each other, their stomachs in close contact, and their cunts touching.

'One moment, Alice!' I exclaimed, just as she was beginning to agitate herself on Fanny. 'Let me see that you are properly placed before you start.'

Leaning over her bottom, I gently parted her thighs, till between them I saw the cunts of the mistress and the maid resting on each other, slit to slit, clitoris to clitoris, half-hidden by the mass of their closely interwoven hairs, The sweetest of sights! Then after restoring her thighs to their original position closely pressed against each other, I gently thrust my right hand between the girls' navels, and worked it along amidst their bellies till it lay between their cunts. 'Press down a bit, Alice,' I said, patting her bottom with my disengaged hand. Promptly she complied with two or three vigorous down-thrusts which forced my palm hard against Fanny's cunt while her own pressed deliciously against the back of my hand. The sensation of thus feeling at the same time these two full fat fleshy warm and throbbing cunts between which my hand lay in sandwich-fashion was something exquisite; and it was with the greatest reluctance that I removed it from the sweetest position it is ever likely to be in. But Alice's restless and involuntary movements proclaimed that she was fast yielding to her feverish impatience to fuck Fanny and to taste the rapture of spending on the cunt of her maid the emission provoked by its sweet contact and friction against her own excited organ.

She still held Fanny closely clasped against her and, with head slightly thrown back, she kept her eyes fixed on her maid's terrified averted face with a gloating hungry look, murmuring softly, 'Fanny, you shall now...love me!' Both the girls were quivering, Alice from overwhelming and unsatisfied lust, Fanny from shame and horrible apprehension.

Caressing Alice's bottom encouragingly, I whispered, 'Go ahead, dear.' In a trice her lips were pressed to Fanny's flushed cheeks on which she rained hot kisses as she slowly began to agitate her cunt against her maid's with voluptuous movements of her beautiful bottom.

'Oh Miss...!' gasped Fanny, her eyes betraying the sexual emotion that she felt beginning to overpower her, her colour coming and going. Quicker and more agitated became Alice's movements; soon she was furiously rubbing her cunt against Fanny's with strenuous down-thrusting strokes of her bottom, continuing her fierce kisses on her maid's cheeks as the latter lay helpless with half-closed eyes and tightly clasped in her mistress's arms. Then a hurricane of sexual rage seemed to seize

Alice. Her bottom wildly oscillated and gyrated with confused jerks, thrusts and shoves as she frenziedly pressed her cunt against Fanny's with a rapid jogging motion. Suddenly Alice seemed to stiffen and become almost rigid; her arms gripped Fanny more tightly than ever. Then her head fell forward on Fanny's shoulder as an indescribable spasm thrilled through her, followed by convulsive vibrations and tremors. Almost simultaneously, Fanny's half-closed eyes turned upwards till the whites were showing and her lips parted. She gasped brokenly, 'Oh...Miss...Alice...Ah...h!' then thrilled convulsively while quiver after quiver shot through her. The blissful crisis had arrived! Mistress and maid were deliriously spending, cunt against cunt. Alice was in rapturous ecstasy at having so deliciously satisfied her sexual desires by means of her maid's cunt, while forcing the latter to spend in spite of herself. While Fanny was quivering ecstatically under heavenly sensations hitherto unknown to her (owing to her having been unconscious when she was ravished) and now communicated to her wondering senses by her mistress, whom she still felt lying on her and in whose arms she was still clasped.

Intently I watched both girls, curious to learn how they would regard each other when they had recovered from their ecstatic trance. Would the mutual satisfaction of their overwrought sexual cravings wipe out the animosity between them which had caused the strange events of this afternoon? Or would Alice's undoubted lust for her maid be simply raised to a higher pitch by this satisfying of her sexuality on her maid's body? And would Fanny consider that she had been violated by her mistress and therefore bear a deeper grudge than ever against her? It was a pretty problem and I eagerly awaited its solution.

Alice was the first to move. With a long-drawn breath indicative of intense satisfaction she raised her head off Fanny's shoulder. The slight movement roused Fanny, who mechanically turned her averted head towards Alice, and as the girls languidly opened their humid eyes, they found themselves looking straight at each other. Fanny coloured like a peony and quickly turned her eyes away. Alice on the contrary continued to regard the blushing face of her maid, a look of gratification and triumph came into her eyes, then she deliberately placed her lips on Fanny's and kissed her, saying softly but significantly: 'Now it's Mr Jack's turn, my dear.' Then raising her head she, with a malicious smile, watched Fanny to see how she would receive the intimation.

Fanny darted a startled, horrified glance at me, another at her mistress, then, seeing that both our faces only confirmed Alice's announcement, she cried pitifully, 'No, no, Mr Jack! No, no, Miss Alice! Oh Miss, how can you be so cruel!' With a malicious smile, Alice again kissed her horrified maid, saying teasingly, 'You must tell us afterwards which you like best, Fanny, and, if you're very good and let Mr Jack have as good a fuck as you have just given me, we'll have each other in front of you for special edification!'

She kissed Fanny once more, then rose slowly off her, exposing as she did so, her own cunt and that of her maid. I shot a quick glance at both in turn. The girls had evidently spent profusely, their hairs glistened with tiny drops of love-dew, while here and there bits were plastered down.

Alice caught my glance and smiled merrily. 'I let myself go, Jack!' she laughed. 'But there will be plenty ready when you are,' she added wickedly. 'I'll just put myself right, then I'll do lady's maid to Fanny and get her ready for you.' Then with a saucy look she whispered, 'Haven't I sketched out a fine programme?'

'You have indeed!' I replied as I seized her and kissed her. 'I wish only that I was to have you first, dear, while I'm so rampant.'

'No, no,' she whispered, kissing me again, 'I'm not ready yet. Fuck Fanny well, Jack! It will do her good, and you'll find her a delicious mover.' And she ran off to her alcove.

I sat down on the couch by Fanny's side and began to play with her breasts, watching her closely. She was in a terrible state of agitation, her head rolling from side to side, her eyes closed, her lips slightly apart, while her bosom heaved wildly. As my hands seized her breasts gently she started, opened her eyes, and seeing that it was me she piteously pleaded, 'Oh Mr Jack, don't... don't...!' She could not bring herself to say the dreadful word that expressed her fate.

'Don't...what, Fanny?' I asked maliciously.

With an effort she brought out the word. 'Oh Sir, don't...fuck me!'

'But your mistress has ordered it, Fanny, and she tells me you are very sweet, and so I want it! And it will be like taking your maidenhead, only much nicer for you, as you won't have the pain that girls feel when they are first ravished, and you'll be able to taste all the pleasure.'

'No, no, Mr Jack!' she cried. 'Don't...fuck me!'

Just then Alice came up with water, a sponge and a towel. 'What's the matter, Jack?' she asked.

'Your maid says she doesn't want to be fucked, dear. Perhaps you can convince her of her foolishness.'

Alice was now sponging Fanny's cunt with sedulous care, and her attentions were making Fanny squirm and wriggle involuntarily in the most lovely fashion, much to her mistress's gratification. When Alice had finished she turned to me and said, 'She's quite ready, Jack. Go ahead!'

'No, no, Sir!' yelled Fanny in genuine terror, but I quickly got between her legs and placed myself on her palpitating stomach, clasping her in my arms, then, directing my prick against her delicious cleft, I got its head inside without much difficulty. Fanny was now wild with fright and shrieked despairingly as she felt me effect an entrance into her. As my prick penetrated her deeper and deeper, she went off into a paroxysm of frantic plungings in the hope of dislodging me.

I did not experience half the difficulty I had anticipated in getting into Fanny, for her spendings under Alice had lubricated the passage; but she was exceedingly tight and I must have hurt her for her screams were terrible. Soon however I was into her till our hairs mingled, then I lay still for a little while to allow her to recover a bit; and before long her cries ceased and she lay panting in my arms.

Alice, who was in my full sight and had been watching with the closest attention and the keenest enjoyment this practical violation of her maid, now bent forward and said softly, 'She's all right, Jack! Go on, dear!' Promptly I set to work to fuck Fanny, at first with long slow piston-like strokes of my prick, then more and more rapid thrusts and shoves, driving myself well up her. Suddenly I felt Fanny quiver deliciously under me...she had spent! Delightedly I continued to fuck her...soon she spent again, then again, and again, quivering with the most exquisite tremors and convulsions as she lay clasped tightly in my arms, uttering almost inarticulate 'ahs' and 'ohs' as the spasm of pleasure thrilled through her.

Now I began to feel my own ecstasy quickly approaching. Hugging Fanny against me more closely than ever I let myself go and rammed furiously into her as she lay quivering under me till the rapturous crisis overtook me, then madly I shot her my pent up torrent of boiling virile balm, inundating her sweetly excited interior and evidently causing her the most exquisite bliss, for her head fell backwards, her eyes closed, her nostrils dilated, her lips parted, as she ejaculated, 'Ah...ah...ah!' when feeling each jet of my hot discharge shoot into her. Heavens, how I spent! The thrilling, exciting and provocative events of the afternoon had worked me up into a such state of sexual excitement that even the ample discharge I had spent into Fanny did not quench my ardour; and as soon as the delirious thrills and spasms of pleasure had died away, I started fucking her a second time.

But Alice intervened. 'No Jack!' she exclaimed softly, adding archly, 'You must keep the rest for me. Get off quickly, dear, and let me attend to Fanny before it is too late.'

Unable to challenge her veto, I reluctantly withdrew my prick from Fanny's cunt, after kissing her ardently, then rose and retired to my alcove, while Alice quickly took Fanny into her charge and attended to her with loving care.

When I returned, Fanny was still lying on her back fastened down to the couch, and Alice was sitting by her and talking to her with an amused smile as she gently played with her maid's breasts. As soon as Fanny caught sight of me she blushed rosy red, while Alice turned and greeted me with a welcoming smile.

'I've been trying to find out from Fanny which fucking she liked the best,' she said with a merry smile, 'but she won't say. Did she give you a good time, Jack?'

'She was simply divine!' I replied as I stooped and kissed her still blushing maid.

'Then we'll give her the reward we promised,' replied Alice, looking sweetly at Fanny, 'she shan't be tied up any more and she'll see you fuck me, Jack, presently. Set her free, Jack!' she added. Soon Fanny rose confusedly from the couch on which she had tasted the probably unique experience of being fucked in rapid succession first by a girl and then by a man. She was very shamefaced and her limbs were very stiff from having been retained so long in one position, but we supported her to the sofa where we placed her between us, then we gently chafed and massaged her limbs till they regained their powers and soothed her with our kisses and caresses. Our hands wandered all over her naked and still trembling body, and soon she was herself again.

'Now, Jack!' exclaimed Alice who was evidently on heat again. 'Are you ready?'

'Look, dear!' I replied, holding up my limp prick for her inspection, adding with a smile, 'Time, my Christian friend!' She laughed, took my prick gently in her hands and began to fondle it, but as it did not show the signs of returning life she so desired to see, she caught hold of Fanny's hand and made it assist hers, much to Fanny's bashful confusion. But her touch had the desired effect, and soon I was stiff and rampant again.

'Thanks, Fanny!' I said as I lovingly kissed her blushing face. 'Now, Alice, if you will!' Quickly Alice was on her back with parted legs. Promptly I got on to her and drove my prick home up her cunt, then, clasping each other closely, we set to work and fucked each other deliciously, till we both spent in delirious transports of pleasure which heightened Fanny's blushes, as with humid eyes she watched us in wondering astonishment and secret delight.

After exchanging ardent kisses we rose. 'Come Fanny, we must dress and be off. I didn't know it was so late!' exclaimed Alice. Off the girls went together to Alice's alcove while I retired to mine. I was delighted that their departure should be thus hurried as it would obviate the possible awkwardness of a more formal leave taking. Soon we all were dressed. I called a taxi and put the girls into it, their faces discreetly veiled; and as they drove off, I felt that the afternoon had not been wasted!

GALLERY V

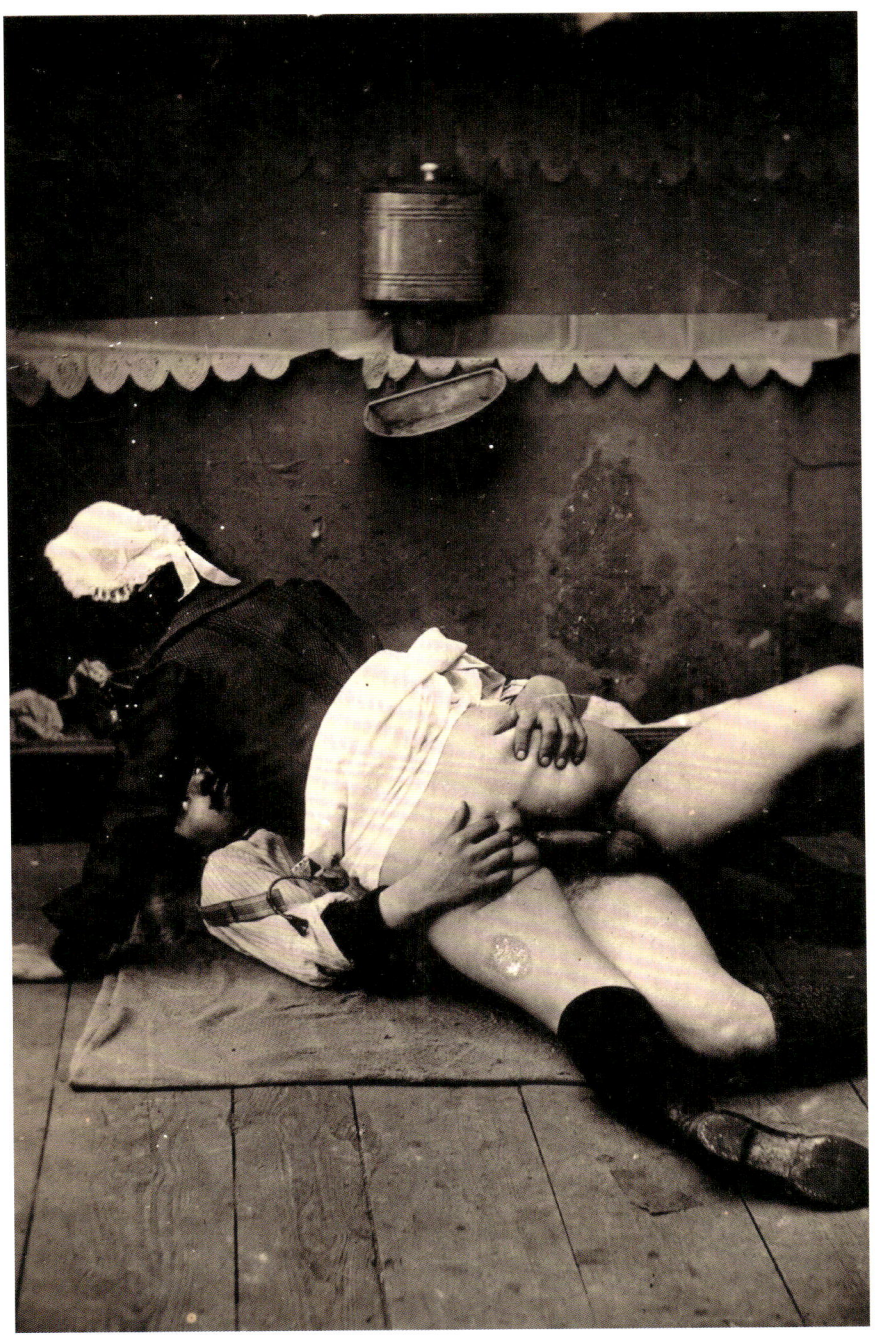

BEATRICE

GORDON GRIMLEY

As far as pastiche Edwardian erotica goes, *Beatrice* is a masterpiece.
Written by Gordon Grimley, who was, among other things, a
surprisingly erudite managing director of *Penthouse International*, this
exquisite literary spoof was first published in 1982 with a suitably
misleading foreword. The plot is vague and inchoate, at times
maddeningly so, but the author manages to convey an atmosphere of
haunting decadence with great success. Aunt Maude's and Katherine's
outrageous treatment of Maria, the maid, her coupling with Frederick
the manservant, as if they were breeding stock, her 'acquiescence' and
her subsequent recruitment as 'stable mistress' in the following extract,
all give an idea of this story's highly original treatment. The opening
sentence to one of *Beatrice's* chapters, 'The days of strangeness closed
in upon us further…', perfectly evokes the institutional atmosphere
and submissive mood that are the background to the eponymous
heroine's bizarre, masochistic experiences.

We took coffee in the lounge, then turned to liqueurs.
There was a festive air. I could feel it. We lounged at our
ease. The shackles were cast. Caroline laughed occasionally with
Uncle. We were tamed.

When the maid brought in the Cointreau, Katherine took
her wrist.

"Drink with us," she said.

"M'am?" the maid's cheeks coloured.

"Drink with us—sit with us—here at my feet—take a glass."
Katherine's words were pellets. They stung against my skin. The
woman skimmed a nervous look around where we sat in a circle.

"Look, I will hold your glass while you sit," Aunt Maude told her.

The maid obeyed at last, discomfited in her sitting on the floor. Her legs coiled under her. I liked the shape of her calves. Her ankles were slender. Slender ankles and plump thighs often betoken sensuousness to some degree.

"Lean back and be comfortable," Aunt Maude said. She dropped a cushion onto the carpet for the maid to lean upon. She looked like a houri—an odalisque. Uncle was whispering to Caroline. What were they saying?

"Attractive women often sit on the floor," Katherine remarked. The maid looked at her and did not know whether to smile or not. Katherine's smile was a cat's smile. With a flip of her toes she kicked off one of the gold Turkish slippers she was wearing and, to the woman's startlement, laid her toes on her thigh. Her toes curled.

"It is nice," Katherine said. Her foot moved upwards along the maid's hip and felt its curving. "Drink your drink," she said sharply. The woman obeyed. My aunt eased a shoe off in turn. Sitting obliquely behind the maid she lifted her leg, eased her stockinged foot beneath the woman's chin and lifted it.

"Lie down—down!" my aunt said.

The maid's arm made a querulous seeking gesture, but she obeyed. The cushion squeezed itself from under her. Katherine circled her leg and moved the sole of her foot lightly over the woman's prominent breasts. She started and would have sat up if Aunt Maude's foot had not then moved with a twist of ankle to the front of her neck.

The maid's eyes bulged.

"M'am—I don't want to," she whined.

"Oh, be quiet!" Katherine said impatiently. Her foot slid back down. Her toes hooked in the hem of the maid's skirt and drew it up above her stocking tops. Plump thighs gleamed. The simple garters she wore bit tightly into her flesh.

"No, please, M'am."

Neither listened. Aunt Maude's toes were caressing her neck

and up behind her ear. Katherine's toes delved upwards beneath
the hang of the upflipped skirt. The woman's hands scrabbled
on the carpet. Mu aunt's toes soothed over her mouth. A choking
little cry and the maid's back arched. The delicate searching
movements of Katherine's toes up between her thighs made
the black material ripple. The maid's cheeks were pink. Her lips
parted beneath the sole of my aunt's foot which rubbed suavely,
skimming her mouth. Katherine's toes projected up into the
skirt. Her heel was rubbing now.

The maid moaned and closed her eyes. Beside me, Caroline
puffed out her breath. The maid's eyes closed. Her bottom
worked slightly. She drew up one knee. My uncle's eyes were
strangely incurious. Aunt Maude slipped down on to her knees
beside the maid and began unbuttoning the front of her dress.
The ripe gourds of her breasts came into view. Her nipples were
stark and thick in their conical rising.

Katherine slid down onto her knees in turn. Her hands swept
the skirt of the maid's dress up to her waist. A bulge of pubic
hairs sprouted thickly. The maid covered her face and made
little cries.

"Open your legs properly!" Katherine told her sharply. Still
with her eyes covered the maid began to edge her ankles apart.
It would be her first such pleasuring, perhaps, though female
servants who shared bedrooms frequently fingered one another.

~

Maria—the maid with whom she and Katherine had toyed—
stayed on. On the morning after her pleasuring she became
more acquiescent and submissive to commands. Her skirts were
hemmed excessively short. Whenever my uncle looked at her
thighs she blushed.

One afternoon we had what my aunt called "an amusement."

At lunch Maria had been complimented upon her serving of the wine and food. She looked foolishly pleased. On our retirement to the drawing room I was intrigued to see a large camera of mahogany and brass standing upon a stout tripod. Its lens faced inwards from the windows, no doubt to gather light. Before it was placed a simple wooden chair. Other furniture had been pressed back against the walls.

Upon Maria's bringing-in of the liqueurs, my aunt said to her, "Maria, we shall take your portrait today—your likeness. Will that not please you?"

Maria smiled and curtsied. "As it please you, M'am," she replied. As I learned afterwards, my uncle had rooted her with his cock the evening before, over the dining room table. She had not struggled unduly, it seemed. Katherine enlivened us by playing on the piano. It was an old melody, sad and wistful. Jenny—who had not lunched with us, having been attending to Amanda upstairs—came and joined us.

"Bring the manservant," Katherine told her.

Jenny disappeared and reappeared. There was a clattering from the distant kitchen while Maria tidied up. Once again Frederick was naked, led by his collar and chain. A blue bow was tied about the root of his penis which hung limp. Jenny led him to the chair and turned him to stand beside it, facing the camera.

Aunt Maude wiped her lips with a lace hanky and went out. A sound of scuffling came—a slap—then a silence. In a minute or two my aunt entered with Maria who wore now open-net stockings, knee boots, a tiny black corset which left her breasts and navel uncovered, and a large feathered hat such as one might see at Ascot. Her face was well adorned with powder and rouge. Her eyes were heavy-lidded.

At the sight of Frederick she started back. A loud smack on her naked bottom quickly corrected her.

"Go and sit in the chair—act as a lady—this is a formal portrait," my aunt told her. My uncle sat with his arms crossed.

The wobbling of Maria's large bottom cheeks as she obeyed absorbed him. Her bush was dark—thick and luxuriant. Hot-cheeked she sat and faced us.

"Cross your legs, Maria—how dare you show yourself!"my aunt snapped at her.

Katherine lit a cigarette. The smoke coiled about us like incense.

Aunt Maude moved to the camera and bent behind it, casting a large black velvet cloth over her head and shoulders, as over the back of the camera itself. Her hand sought forward and focussed the big brass lens. Maria's eyes had a sullen look. Aunt Maude took one slide of the pair, cautioning them to be still for a full minute. Then my uncle rose and assisted her in changing the glass plates.

"Raise your right hand, Maria, and let his prick lie on your palm!" Katherine said.

There was hesitation. Imperceptibly Fredericks prick stirred and thickened as it lay on Maria's warm, moist hand. Maria would have bitten her lip in dismay if my aunt had not told her sharply to keep her expression fixed in a smile.

With small variations Aunt Maude continued photographing. The light was excellent, she observed. By the fourth attempt Frederick's prick stemmed fully upright, the flesh swelling around and above the neat blue bow. Maria was forced to hold it now. Her face had a dull, vapid look.

"It is done," Aunt Maude said at last. She collected the heavy glass plates together. They would be framed in gilt, she said.

"I will take them now," Katherine said. Walking across to Frederick whose penis had not lost its fine erection, she took hold of his chain. "Get up," she said quietly to Maria. She smiled across at me. Did she know I wanted her?

"Where shall you take them?"Aunt Maude asked.

"To the stable. It is time they were coupled." A short squeal came from Maria as Katherine moved behind her and inserted a finger upwards between the globing cheeks of her bottom. "So tight and plump—she will milk him deeply," she smiled. Her smile had a taste of olives.

Maria jerked forward and went to kneel at my aunt's feet.

"M'am, I beg you!" she pleaded.

Katherine clicked her fingers and Jenny came forward with a leather neckband and chain which she secured quickly around Maria's neck.

My aunt's eyes were kindly. She gazed down at the top of Maria's bent head.

"Beg me you should, Maria. What a foolish woman you are." Her hands raised her skirt. The dark vee of her pubis was apparent to all our eyes through her white, split drawers. Her bared thighs came warm and sleek to Maria's face. Maria lifted her head slowly. Her tongue emerged, mouth hovering about the plump mound whose curls sprouted so thickly. The lips moved against her lips. My aunt's legs spread a little. Maria's tongue made a broad wet smudge around her pouting.

"Rise now!" my aunt said to her. The chain clinked. Jenny pulled on it and drew the woman to her feet.

"M'am…" Maria's lips quivered. She looked like an overgrown girl who did not know what to do. Her nipples protruded thickly on her large, milky breasts. The surrounding circles were broad, crinkly. The flesh was firm.

"You will obey, Maria. Mare and stallion in the stable—it is fitting. Go now!" Aunt Maude ordained.

Katherine led them out. Through the windows I could see the trio crossing the lawn towards the paddock.

Aunt Maude turned to us. "Go upstairs," she said, "you should not have watched."

~

My immediate concern was with Amanda. She had dallied long in the garden with Caroline. Nevertheless, their would-be pleasing efforts were evident from the array of blooms which stood on the kitchen table.

Maria was adjusting some of them. She gazed at me rather shyly as I entered.

"You are happy, Maria?" I asked. The bloom of health seemed indeed to be upon her. I had a certain taste for the voluptuousness of her curves which her deliberately tight and abbreviated costume enhanced. She nodded. A veil of uncertainty was in her eyes. Her fingers flustered at the flowers. There was a new ring on her finger, I noticed. It was one of no great account. My uncle had given it to her, I guessed. On my questioning her, she confessed it.

"He mounted you, Maria?"

The question was so direct that she knew not what to answer. A tiny bubble of saliva appeared between her lips which were richly curved but smallish.

"As Frederick did in the stable, Maria?" I insisted. Beneath her black skirt I could envisage the ripeness of her cheeks in their waiting.

"My husband don't know, M'am," she stammered.

"Answer the questions, Maria," I said softly and stayed her hands from their toying with the stalks of the blooms. Her palms were moist.

"I was ashamed, M'am," she choked. The expression in her eyes was ill-disguised. It followed not the twisting of her lips. She would lend herself, I sensed, to whatever I intended.

"Did you buck or struggle, Maria?" I gripped the bun of her hair which was coiled up with hairpins. One loosened and fell between my fingers.

"No, M'am, I daren't. Miss Katherine she had the whip, in the stable, and the Mistress she warned me not to move afterwards when I was in the dining room over the table."

I was but half listening. Though not indolent, she was learning her pleasures in the sly way known to such women. An occasional protest cleared her conscience, as she saw it.

Her husband, she said, was a good man, a quiet man, like herself nearing thirty. He worked as a farm labourer.

I released her hair.

"You will come shortly into my sevice, Maria—as also your husband. There will be work for him to do around the house. I am having a site cleared for stables. You may perhaps be my Stable Mistress, and it so please me. You have learned a little of the handling of females and you are acquiescent. You will learn under my instructions."

I doubted whether she knew the meaning of "acquiescent" any more than she would have recognised a five-pound note. I have since given field-girls a guinea piece for their intended services and seen them gaze at it in wonder.

Words unspoken danced upon Maria's lips. From the brief description she had given me of her husband, Ned, he would be amply able to service both Caroline and Jenny when required. Maria—given over to such pleasures as I occasionally permitted her—would soon grow used to it.

GALLERY VI

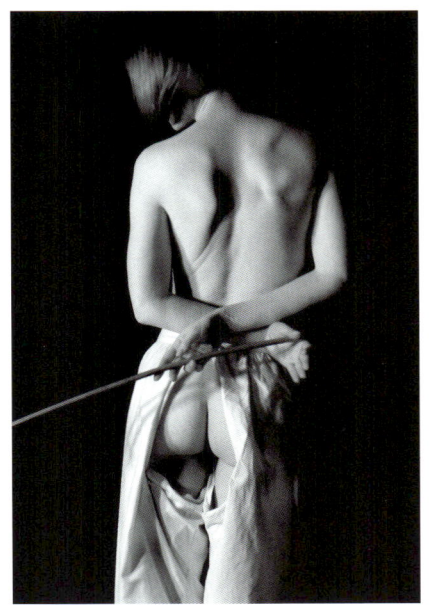

CHINA HAMILTON

ALICE & HER FRIEND

CHINA HAMILTON

China Hamilton is an internationally famous photographer. His
photographic work is the subject of several monographs and is also
included in many anthologies. A less well-known aspect of China's
talented and restless imagination is his short fiction writing. The mood
of brooding authority that he so brilliantly evokes in his photography
is echoed in his prose, and here we are fortunate enough to have a
sample of both genres.

Alice and Rosemary were the same age and grew up together
in an orphanage. It was 1843, and by the standards
of the time, it had been a reasonable place. Privately and
philanthropically run, it tried to show some compassion for its
inmates. True, their bare bottoms had frequent encounters with
Matron's birch twigs, and true they worked at endless and boring
tasks while there was light from the stained glass windows. But
they had shoes, beds and plain food. They learnt to read and
write and above all, the girls learnt to serve, for that was their
destiny decreed by the Bible. They studied the Bible on Sundays.

So it was that Alice and Rosemary were groomed for
domestic service. So good was their training that the orphanage
held a reputation in society as a place to acquire good young
staff who would give no trouble and knew their duties. At the
age of fourteen, they were both selected for positions in the
same house. It was at that moment that they were given the
Christian names of Alice and Rosemary. It was of no account
what their real names were, their new employer decided, as they

stood before her. Alice and Rosemary suited them and it suited the employer.

For these two fourteen-year-olds, it was a strict but reasonable house to work for and they grew both in age and experience as they practiced their skills and duties. They became used to the endless tasks that stretched from early fire-lighting to late evening duties. There was fun though in the kitchen with a happy and generous cook, so they ate well and grew into strong and attractive girls. They enjoyed their one Sunday a month off, when they could walk in the park and get cheeked by the young men. They had slept together and cuddled together in the orphanage and though they now had separate single cots in the attic of the house, their stirring hormones led them to extend their loving friendship and explore the wonders of each others' bodies, climbing boldly into each others arms at night.

Things changed when this hardworking but comfortable household had to uproot and leave for India where the Colonel had to serve with his Regiment. There was no place for Alice and Rosemary, who were now eighteen. Honest and good though their service had been, they would be out on the street, armed only with a good reference. By chance, the Colonel's wife was asked by an acquaintance what she would do with her staff and so, because of this contact, the two girls made an arduous journey to new employment in the West Country.

They were collected by coach in town. Their hearts fell as the final part of the journey went on and on across increasingly desolate land. A bitter, grim-faced man was at the reins, huddled in his greatcoat. He ignored every question they asked him.

At last they passed through the gates and approached the house up a long, tree-lined drive. An immense park surrounded them. The house was massive and bleak and it loomed out of an evening mist. They entered through the servants' door as darkness fell. A housekeeper, dressed in black with a large bunch of keys hanging from her leather belt, took them in her charge. There was something ominous about this woman. She seemed more suited to a house of correction than this benighted place. She led them up narrow back stairs to a cold bedroom with iron beds and one small window. On each bed was laid out a full set of maid's cloths, complete with pairs of starched drawers.

'Get out of your travelling clothes and get dressed in the uniforms,' said the housekeeper.

She stood to one side of the room, which was lit by a single candle, waiting silently while each girl nervously undressed. They were acutely aware that they would need to be completely naked in front of her. They were conscious that her hard eyes took in every detail of their bodies. In their embarrassment, they hurried to cover themselves. At last they stood dressed.

'Downstairs to the kitchen, where cook will give you supper. You will have no duties tonight except to be inspected by the master and the mistress. You will be called when that is to happen. You will only wear the clothes that are provided for you, including underwear, while you work here,' said the housekeeper.

In the kitchen, the cook fed them well. There were no other staff to be seen. They sat by the fire waiting for the summons. It came at last, and a spotty youth in footman's livery escorted them through long dark corridors. They saw the mistress, Lady Elizabeth, first. She was a most attractive woman in her mid-30s, yet she had something about her that was chilling. She spoke slowly, measuring each word. She started by making the girls turn round and show themselves from all sides. She seemed neither pleased nor displeased with them.

'We are a small household, as we only use part of this wretched house. We have been without maids for a time so there will be much to do to catch up. Mrs Weeks, the housekeeper, will instruct you in such matters. You have come with good references,' she said. 'His Lordship and I have a distrust of young girls. They have their heads in the clouds, run after young men, and do slovenly work. I'm sure you have come from one of those lax and modern homes. London is like that. Here we do things more effectively. Any little failures in your demeanour or duties and we will have Weeks brisk you up in the punishment room. I hope you understand me clearly on that score?'

Alice and Rosemary, bowed their heads, nodded and murmured abject agreements.

'Now his Lordship needs to see over you,' she said. 'Leave now, the boy will show you.'

She turned back to her embroidery.

His Lordship was a swarthy man, not a great deal older that his wife. He was stood in the study by a roaring fire, a full glass and decanter to hand. He waved them in, lined them up before him and contemplated them in silence.

At last he spoke, after slowly sipping from his glass. 'Well, well, well, what do we have here. A couple of prize young hens if ever I've seen a pair. Her Ladyship won't like you two, I'll be bound. Doesn't like attractive young girls. You better get used to her punishment room, she is fond of it. Her and Weeks.'

He sipped again, warming to his task. He asked each their names, making them step forward and give him a little curtsey. Alice and Rosemary relaxed a little and tried to smile.

'I'm going to be blunt, because I'm a blunt man,' he said. 'I like a lot of things, dogs, horses, shooting game, shooting poachers, a little fishing. But in particular, I like a nice young girl. Even better, I like two nice young girls, if you get my drift? I expect you to visit me and accommodate my needs when I send for you. I'll make it plain, it will be part of your duties. You will keep the matter to yourselves and you might as well accept it with good grace and a smile. If you don't, I'll please my wife and send you packing with no references. Worse, I might report you to the constable for theft. Not a pretty set of alternatives. So you be sensible and we will all get along fine.'

His manner hardened as he had moved on to the threats. Alice and Rosemary were dumb struck. Even though they were in no sense worldly, they understood the gist of his Lordship's demands for their additional duties. He had indeed been blunt. All they could do was say, 'Yes sir, we will do our best.'

Back in their room with its one candle, they held each other tightly and cried. It was a dreadful place from which they could see there was no escape. Sleep came slowly as their minds dwelt, over and over, upon the events of the evening.

The following day, things seemed a little more normal, though still less than pleasant. The household seemed to consist of the old groom who had been the driver on their arrival. The young lad called Tom, who was footman and everything else. The indifferent cook who kept herself to herself, and the frightening Weeks. There was one other, who kept herself detached from the rest of the servants and that was her ladyship's maid. She was a mature, dowdy woman who spent her time sewing and attending to her ladyship's personal needs. This maid appeared only at meal times and then scuttled off to the upper floors of the house. It was a sad and dark place, bitter as the wind that perpetually blew from the moors above the old house.

Each girl blessed the fact that they had each other, for company and support. Weeks roused them early and set them to doing fires and cleaning grates. Though she was cold, she was reasonable in dealing with their many questions as to where things could be found. She seemed grateful that two hard working pairs of hands had arrived at last.

Alice and Rosemary, lapsed into a tacit acceptance of their lot. The days went by and they soon became used to the place and their duties. Neither master nor mistress seemed to notice them and, except for the occasional instruction, no words passed between them. Even the cook started to make conversation, and the boy Tom, when alone with them, made earnest attempts to please the girls with silly jokes.

One afternoon Rosemary was laying out tea for her ladyship. The silver teapot slipped from her grasp, and fell onto the Turkish rug spraying tea in all directions from lid and spout.

'Stupid child,' said her ladyship. 'Get it cleared up and bring me fresh tea.' That was all she said. Rosemary called for Alice to help, equilibrium was restored and her Ladyship had her tea.

As Rosemary curtseyed before leaving the room, the ominous words came to her ears: 'You'll be brisked up tonight. Now leave.'

Weeks, when told, seemed very detached about the matter. The night came.

'I'm surprised that both of you have made it this far without a visit to the special room my girl,' she said to Rosemary as they walked together up a staircase in the old, unused part of the house. The way was lit by a candle that Weeks held. When they reached the top, a door on the dusty landing stood open and light came from inside. The two of them entered.

The mistress was already there, sitting calmly on a large chair. The room was well lit by wall mounted candles. Rosemary, somewhat in a daze, took in the room. It had once, she saw, been a boudoir. Now it was bare with a few chairs and, in the centre, a wooden construction like a saw-horse but on longer legs. Its top came to an edge which was minimally padded by old, well-stained leather. Each leg fitted with leather straps. Upon one wall, she noticed, there hung an array of instruments of flagellation. Small whips, leather straps and a number of long canes.

'Now girl,' said Weeks. 'Best if you go along with this and get it over with. Just do as I tell you and all will be fine. Slip off your pinafore and dress and be smart about it.'

Rosemary did as she was told, folding the clothes with deliberate neatness onto a chair. She now stood before the two women in her undergarments.

'Have the girl strip to the waist, Weeks, if you please. Don't want her sweating into the good clothes my money provides,' said Lady Elizabeth.

'Off with your top,' said the Housekeeper and Rosemary obeyed, slipping off the simple white chemise to expose her young breasts.

'Have her mount the horse,' said the mistress.

Weeks pulled forward a small wooden box and placed it underneath the horse.

'Climb astride the horse, girl, use the box,' she said.

Rosemary, stood up on the box and swung her leg over the ridge to stand with her legs apart across its edge.

'Come down a little toward the end and then part your draws and sit down with your bare cunny on the top. I will do the rest,' said Weeks.

Rosemary did as she was told and parted the material to place her sweet place with its brown curls upon the old leather which was marked by the sex of many before her.

Satisfied that the girl was correctly positioned, her bare cunt pressing down against the hard leather top of the saw-horse, Weeks quickly pulled away the box and Rosemary now felt the painful and instant discomfort of the leather forcing open her labia. Quickly Weeks swept up each booted ankle and strapped it high up upon the rear leg of the horse so that Rosemary was seated like a jockey. She then pulled the girl down at the front till her nipples caressed the top of the horse. Each of the girl's wrists was now strapped low down on the front legs. Rosemary was now perfectly placed, bottom up and ready, the edge pressing cruelly on the base of her mound and her clitoris. She now understood the cunning of this sadistic device to add additional suffering and pain.

Weeks proceeded to bare the bottom. She pulled open the division of the drawers and worked the material back, tucking it under so that each neat, tightened cheek was clearly on show and gleaming pink in the candle light.

'Now Week's, there's a good sight. What a suitable bottom the young Miss has. Well rounded and pert, ripe for a brisking. Such fresh young skin, neglected for so long. We must make her do her duties without carelessness. A good cane, Weeks, best for a tight little bottom. That one, the third from the end. That will get her working on the horse, give her a good ride.'

It was the first time that her Ladyship had shown any sign of animation or interest. Her cheeks had something of a flush and her languid voice had become excited. Weeks took up the suggested cane and flexed it a few times to get its measure. She then positioned herself to use it on the proffered bottom. While this had been going on, Rosemary had tried to keep quiet, but the growing pain between her legs had made her whimper.

'Two dozen if you please, Weeks, we must make up for neglect and mark that virgin skin a little. Keep them in a tight group, she has a small arse. Not too hurried, strike just below the curve, you know the spot I'm sure. Now off you go.'

Rosemary had known the burning pain of the birch on many occasions during her time in the orphanage. That was a long time ago and while the birch twigs had been painful, they in no way matched the extraordinary pain of each stroke of the cane. Weeks was obviously skilled at this task and laid the strokes one upon another to the lower part of the rounded cheeks. At each stroke Rosemary could not help but drive forward and punish her crotch. 'Working upon the horse,' as the Mistress had said. After a number of strokes, Rosemary started to shudder and the muscles of her buttocks engaged in involuntary spasms. With each whistle of the cane, and its frightening crack upon the naked flesh came the attendant, pitiful scream of the punished girl. The pause between strokes was full of heavy breathing and sobs.

Lady Elizabeth sat upright upon her chair, hands tightly clasped, rocking slowly with ill-concealed delight as the beating progressed. Her eyes were fixed and bright, looking intensely upon the scene, relishing, quite unashamedly, this act of sadism. There was clear disappointment when the allotted number strokes were finished. She quickly rose from her chair and left the room.

'The girl may have two days off to let the bleeding stop before she goes back to work. We do not want her garments soiled,' she said, as she left.

Rosemary was near fainting, sobbing uncontrollably, unable to support her body any longer. Weeks, methodically wiped the cane on a cloth before hanging it back on its hook on the wall.

Alice did her best to comfort her friend when they were alone in their bedroom. She was distressed when shown what she was familiar with as a sweet posterior to kiss and caress. It was now a black and purple bottom with the raised ridges of the wheals through which little drops of blood still seeped. Weeks had provided an old towel for the girl to protect the bed clothes, though there was no chance of her lying bottom down for some time to come.

Alice knew that it would be only a short period before Lady Elizabeth found a spurious reason to break in another girl to the ways of her house. And so she was even more careful to apply herself to her own duties, especially as she had a double load to accommodate for a few days to come. Three days later, Rosemary was up and about again, though still very much in pain from the rubbing of her clothing. On that third night though, both maids were summoned late to attend the master.

His Lordship was again in his study, warming by the fire and sipping brandy. He was dressed now in a long quilted dressing gown that hung down to his slippered feet. When Tom had shut the door behind them, he waved them forward to come close to him.

'Which of you two pretty things had to visit my wife's little play room?' he asked.

'It was Rosemary,' said Alice, pointing to her friend.

'Ah, yes indeed,' said his Lordship. 'It would be you first, the little, slim, shy one. Just her Ladyship's taste I'm sure. Now

Rosemary, be a good girl and slip off your dress, so that I may see what sort of job Weeks did. Come girl, off with your dress.'

Alice looked horrified and Rosemary went quite white. She though, started the process of undressing there being no alternative but to comply with her Master. As the garments were removed she placed them on a chair until she stood before his Lordship in her white underclothes. He turned to Alice.

'You there girl, what's your name?'

'Alice, sir,' said Alice.

'Yes, Alice. Nice name for a wench. Keep your friend company and slip off your dress as well. I like to compare a fresh bottom with one that's incurred her Ladyship's interests. Come girl don't hesitate, get off that dress.'

Alice, reddened, yet had no alternative but to do as she was told. His Lordship now watched the more curvaceous Alice undress down to her underwear. He now had them both innocently posed before him. He savoured the moment and sipped his drink, nodding in appreciation.

'See that table there.' He pointed to a massive oak table on one side of the room. ' Both of you be good girls and oblige me by going to that table and bending yourselves over it.'

Then as an after thought he added, 'Just to make things pleasant, both slip off your tops, so that I have the pleasure of inspecting you there. I like to see the cut of my young female servants.'

One button at a time, Rosemary and Alice slowly undid their cheap, cotton tops. They slipped them off and let the warm yellow light of the candles play across their breasts. Rosemary's were smaller and tipped up to form dark cheeky ends. Alice's were full and round with large, pink areolas and soft nipples.

'There's a fine sight, something for all tastes. I'll come to those in a while but for now, bend over the table for me.' The two maids did as they were told, resting their warm bosoms upon the cold wood.

The Master rose from his armchair and approached the pair of knickered posteriors. He went first to Alice and after a moment's hesitation, slipped both his hands into the division of her tightened drawers. He slowly pulled them open, exposing the naked flesh beneath. When both cheeks were on show, he felt them with the palms of his hands, caressing their firmness. Without a word, he now moved to Rosemary and repeated the same thing. This time, he traced the wheals and wounds with his fingertips, pressing until he made the girl cry out a little.

'Nothing like a good, heavy cane for a young girl's rump. That cold-hearted vixen Weeks surely knows her trade with such an implement. What a neat small arse you have, girl, almost like a boy's.' His fingers edged between the division of Rosemary's cheeks and a finger pushed into her puckered hole.

'Nice and tight. What a pleasure that will be.'

He stepped back. 'Up you get a moment. Alice, you stay down.' Rosemary stood up and turned to face him.

'Let's have a look at these titties.'

He now proceeded to feel each breast in turn. The cold table had hardened her nipples so that they stood up. He lingered, tweaking each teat in turn between his finger and his thumb, while Rosemary shivered a little, head bowed, not daring to look him in the eye. She was then told to resume her bent over position and he turned his attention to Alice. She now had her breasts examined and teased. At last she also was returned to the table. His Lordship left them there while he went to a small cabinet, from which he withdrew a jar. Putting the jar down between them, he now reached round, beneath the waist and undid the cord tie of Rosemary's knickers. This done, he eased them down. She was now full exposed and naked.

'Part your legs, shy little Rosemary,' he said.

She obeyed, shuffling her black boots on the carpet until her legs were as open as far as her drawers permitted.

'Good girl, sensible to be obedient.'

From within his dressing gown, his Lordship now exposed his erect penis. It stood out, its large head glinting in the light, already a little wet. Rosemary knew nothing of this development but remained frozen in fear over the table. The master fingered Rosemary's cunt. Finding it wet between the curls, he smiled with approval and dipped the head of his prick in the moist nest and pulled it out well lubricated. He now opened the jar and applied the oily cream, working it into the maid's anus. Satisfied, he wet himself again and then rubbed his penis tip against the girl's rear passage. With one forceful thrust of his hips he entered her. Rosemary, arched her back and cried out with surprise and pain, as her nerves fired up with this sudden intrusion. He took no notice but pulled aside his dressing gown to expose his own naked body and then entered Rosemary fully, until his balls banged against the rear of her vulva. The girl screamed, as his body, at each impact, punished again her bruised buttocks.

He reached forward and grabbed her breasts, one in each hand. As his hips pounded he tortured the small bosom with harsh squeezing fingers, stretching and twisting the tender nipples. His body bent over her, kept her upon the table which provide an unyielding edge to her thighs so that there was no reprieve from the deep penetration.

When her cries became weaker and her movements calmer, he at last withdrew, letting her naked form sink slowly down to the floor. Alice had witnessed this sodomising of her dear friend. She had not known what to do. And fear of this man kept her from trying to intervene. His Lordship, though, reasserted his authority and gave two hard slaps to Alice's bottom. He stripped down her knickers as he had done with Rosemary and, far more harshly forced his fingers deep into her sex.

'You're the proud one with spirit, not yet curbed by a taste of the cane. What a nice cunt you have, all wet and dripping, soaking and greedy. I hope you didn't think I would leave you out of the fun. What a fine arse, so round, plenty of space for a dog whip. I'll suggest it to her Ladyship.'

He slapped her cheeks again to emphasise his point, leaving red hand prints. His fingers pushed inside again, making Alice squeal and cry.

'Still a little virgin I see, so tight up there for my tool.'

Grabbing Alice's hips, he forced himself into her sex. It parted and opened till he was against the flesh of her bottom. With rhythmic strokes he took her, hurting her breasts as he had done to Rosemary, and enjoying her cries and protestations. He did not come inside her, for he did not want to risk her becoming pregnant. Instead he withdrew and sprayed his seed across her bottom and bare back.

Time passed, and the girls fell into a dark routine. It was as though the house, and the wild moor above, broke their youthful and innocent nature, to replace it instead with one of grudging acceptance of their lot. For they were after all slaves in a world of absolute power. Their bottoms toughened to the cane and their private places accepted the entry of their Lord and master. Knowing as he did, that one or other of them would suffer again as he beat his hips against their freshly punished bottom.

As one once remarked to the other, in the world as it was, it would be much worse if they did not have a domestic position. As long as they pleased, they would keep their jobs as maids and wear their smart white aprons. They were therefore both determined to please both mistress and master. On that they were very clear.

GALLERY VII

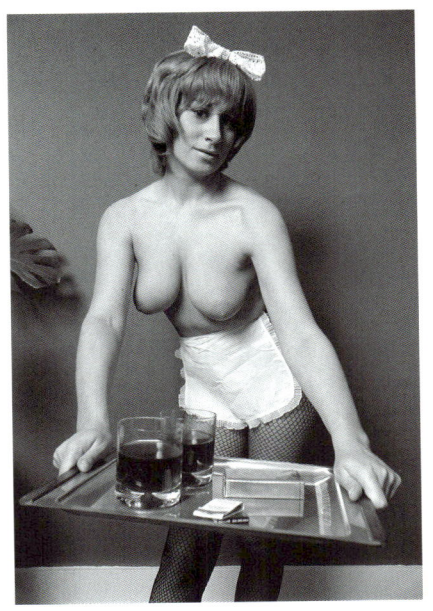

ERIC WILKINS

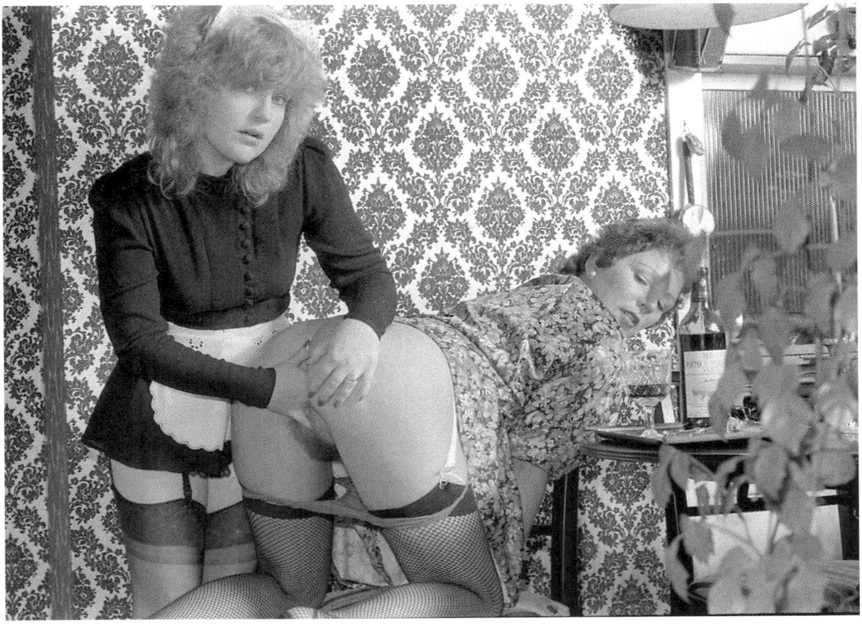

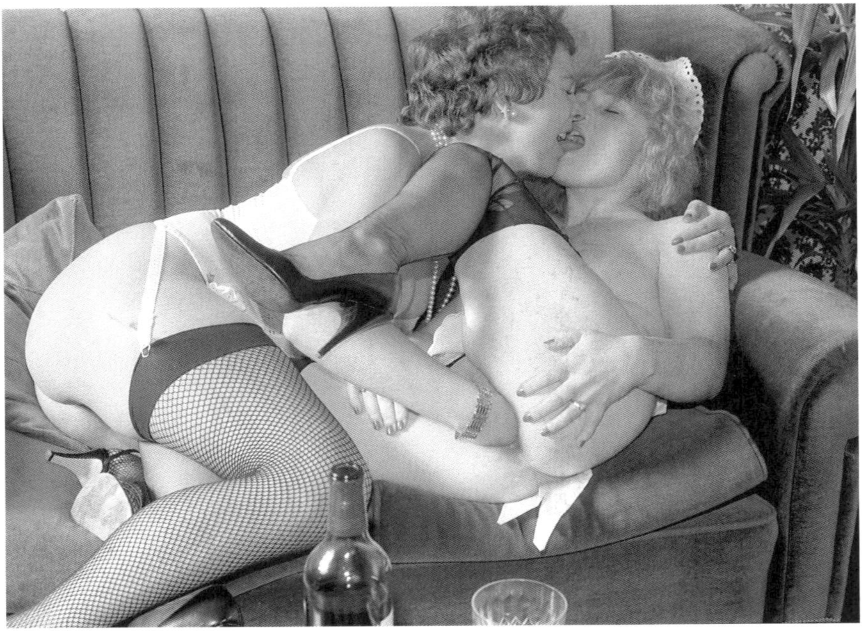

MORNING BATH

HENRI BRETON

Henri Breton is the author of The Devil's Whisper.

'**A**re you coming then, Aunt Mary? The children are ready.'
For the last five years, ever since it had been opened
to the public, it had been an annual pilgrimage, the visit to the
Manor. Molly wasn't sure if she wanted to go. She was over
seventy now. Going back to the Manor stirred her up and it took
a long time to calm down, although her niece could not know
that. All that her niece knew was that she had worked there 'in
service' and she thought it brought back happy memories, the
golden days. Perhaps she would force herself to go upstairs,
since the bedrooms had recently been redecorated and were
now part of the general tour of the house. She would stand
behind the rope with the others, and peer in to the bedroom
that was once as familiar to her as it was to its owner, Lady
Granger. In that room, more than any other, she had dusted
every surface, polished every piece of furniture and vacuumed
the carpets. She had made the bed with fresh linen every week,
put new towels in the bathroom, changed the flowers in the vase
every day, tidied the stack of books on the bedside table. She
would confront the past.

'That's her now,' said Cook.

The bell had rung at a quarter to nine, just the same as it did every morning in the week, and Molly occasionally wondered why the Mistress even bothered. It would make more sense if she just went up there, knocked on the door, opened it, picked up the heavy breakfast tray and enter the Mistress's bedroom. Molly was a practical, sensible girl, always looking for short cuts in life. Well, it was how you got things done, wasn't it?

'Just a minute,' said Cook, as Molly was adjusting the white cap and the ribbons of her pinafore to make sure that they were straight, 'there's that new honey she wanted…'

The tray's progress was halted and its cargo of breakfast (hot coffee, hot milk and warm toast, butter and marmalade), china (pale blue Wedgewood teapot, cup and saucer, milk jug, sugar bowl, jam pot and butter dish), silverware (toast rack, teaspoon, knife, butter knife), newspaper and linen (tray-doily and napkin, pressed and neatly folded) added to.

Cook cut the honeycomb carefully in two and Molly watched as she lifted one dripping, oozing half and gently eased it into a second Wedgewood jam pot. Honeypot, Molly corrected herself. She thought of the other meaning to that word. That's what George calls my private parts. She tried hard not to let another word pop into her mind. His fingers dipping. Slippery. Dripping. Fanny. Oh dear. There it was. And she'd go on thinking about her fanny all the way up the polished, gleaming staircase. She set the tray down on the table outside the door and knocked.

When she heard the vague response, muffled by the solid mahogany door, Molly turned the gleaming brass doorknob, which she polished with Brasso every week, picked up the tray and took it into Mistress's bedroom.

Mistress lay in bed.

'Good morning, M'lady.'

Molly always thought that addressing her employer in this way was old-fashioned, like in a fairytale. But in this house, that's what you called the Mistress. M'lady.

''Morning, Molly. And how are we this morning?'

It was a rhetorical question, blithely asked, and Molly knew better than to answer it. She just smiled brightly, instead, which as far as Lady Granger was concerned, was a perfectly satisfactory response. Indeed, the exchanges between Molly and her employer were never more than a few words. 'Put it over there, please Molly,' or 'Yes, I've finished with that, thank you Molly,' and 'That'll be all, thank you, Molly'. There was never an invitation to share any thoughts or opinions, and Molly preferred it that way, for she really had nothing of any interest to say to the woman. However in the last few weeks Mistress had altered the rules of this laconic exchange. She had asked after Molly's mother who also used to work here, aeons ago. She had remarked approvingly upon Molly's new hairstyle, shorter than before. Enquired about her 'young man', George. And just the other day she had looked at her maid in a funny, critical way, as if making some sort of abrupt appraisal, and then said, in her clipped, clear voice, 'Why Molly! You're really a pretty young thing, you know. Very pretty indeed. But don't let it go to your head.'

Mistress fixed her large grey eyes on Molly's. She noticed that Mistress's nipples were prominent under the thin cotton of her nightdress. Sometimes they were, sometimes they weren't. It was a small detail that made the otherwise identical routine slightly different, a little more interesting. Molly thought she must be the same age as her mum, only her mum looked much older, with harsh lines around her mouth and crow's feet, too. Molly's mum laughed a lot and Lady Granger hardly ever did. She smiled, instead.

Molly was uncertain if this subtle shift in their relationship was a good thing or not. She liked looking at Mistress, who had the appearance of a film star, with her immaculate dark gold hair, delicate, thoroughbred features, huge eyes and perfectly proportioned limbs. And she liked looking at Mistress in her bath. That was usually when she picked up the tray an hour later. The bathroom adjoined the bedroom and always seemed a waste of space to Molly, who lived in a cottage with her parents and three siblings. It was a rectangular room, with the bath at one end, set against a big, single window that looked onto the garden below. The walls were finished in dark green hessian, with gold-framed mezzotints of pastoral scenes. Light flooded through the window, illuminating the bather *contre jour*. Like a picture the Lady was, thought Molly, framed by the window. Molly didn't know why the breakfast tray always ended up in the bathroom, but it did. Right from the very first day Molly had started working at the Manor. Mistress in her bath, pretty as a picture, breakfast tray on the dressing-table near to hand. Mistress reading, on fine days with the strong sun playing on her golden hair, her small breasts uplit by the light reflected from the newspaper.

Sometimes Molly wondered about Mistress now that her husband wouldn't be coming back. How did she… what did she do about… the physical side of love? Did she bring herself off? Molly was curious. She had tried that, under the bedclothes, but it wasn't much fun. Well, it wasn't bad, just not nearly as good as when George brought her off with his fingers or, even better, with his tongue and lips. She liked it when George went down there and serviced her. It was making her wet to think about it, right here and now in Mistress's bathroom. She thought of George and those snuffling, grunting sounds he made; like one of Dan Burridge's porkers he was, snout in the trough at feeding time, such an animal, she thought. He loved it, he did. She would run her fingers through his thick, coarse hair as he kissed and sucked her wet hairy fanny, making such a meal of it, looking up at her bright-eyed and grinning, his mouth and chin all shiny with her juices. She wouldn't let him go any further, though, and she would usually 'finish' him by hand while he felt her breasts. Very occasionally, as a treat, she would suck him off.

She stared down at the part of the pale, immaculate body that was partly submerged in the greenish, clear water. It was so perfect it was almost featureless, she thought, and yet, the whole pleased her in a way she couldn't quite explain. Her eyes were drawn down from Mistress's breasts, her pink nipples (very hard, she could see) the pink areolas, past the waterline to the swell of her little belly, the tiny cave of her bellybutton and her… fanny. Mistress's fanny was what always really fascinated her. Its bush was a light sandy colour and the water was so clear and so nearly still that it seemed she could see each individual hair floating, waving gently like the weed in the stream under the bridge by the almshouses. Mistress's outer lips were clearly visible and also pink. There was the little hood of the clitoris where they joined at the top and below that, protruding only slightly from their big sisters, were the delicate, coral-coloured inner lips. As she stared, she could not prevent herself from wondering what they would be like to touch, whether they would feel as dainty and soft as they looked. She wondered, even, what sort of meal her George would make of them.

An admonitory rustle of the newspaper brought her back to her senses.

Mistress shifted her position slightly in the bath.

'Molly, be a dear – my soap has slipped in. Could you possibly just reach in and…? I do so hate getting the paper wet.' Her voice leisurely, drawling.

Mistress gave Molly a strange, uncertain smile as she said this. Molly didn't know what to think. It was as if Mistress had read her very thoughts. Now she could see where the soap lay; just under her left thigh where it joined her torso, slowly dissolving and surrounded by a little cloud of its own making. If she put her hand there, she could touch Mistress's fanny without it appearing intentional. Molly blushed. Or rather, she flushed, for it was a sudden little rush of pleasure and excitement, more than embarrassment, that had brought the colour to her cheeks.

'Yes, certainly, M'lady,' she tried to say breezily. But it came out as a croak.

She knelt down by the bath and, undoing the buttons of her cuff, carefully rolled up her sleeve. The water felt hot, almost too hot, at first. The back of her hand brushed against the very soft skin of Mistress's inner thigh. There was the soap, but somehow it slipped further back, and now she could feel the gentle tickle from the hair of Mistress's bush against the back of her hand.

She looked up at Mistress, and that was when it all happened at once. Mistress returned Molly's gaze with her big, serious grey eyes and then, with a speed that was almost reptilian, seized Molly's wrist in a light grip, pressing it tenderly against her yielding sex.

Molly shut her eyes. It didn't feel right to return Mistress's gaze. She felt, with her fingers, the soap slip away once more. She felt the silky bush, the outer lips and, between them, even under water, the slipperiness made by Mistress's fanny-juice; this caused her almost giggle, although it was thrilling, too. Mistress was wet, and she was wet in the other way, too. It was clear by Lady Granger's impulsive action that Molly's fingers had permission to explore, and they did so. They carefully parted the inner lips, Molly's eyes still shut, her mind racing and reeling with the thrill of it all. Everything was suddenly reduced to sensations, the smooth enamel of the bath, the warmth of the water, the alien textures of Mistress's intimate parts, the scent of lavender that Mistress liked as a bath essence, the thick pile of the carpet beneath her knees.

Molly always felt herself whenever she took a bath, washed herself down there, and knew every mound and crevice, every fold and pucker. Thus it was that what she felt now seemed both strange and familiar at once, and it was also outrageous and yet perfectly natural that she should slide first one, then two fingers into Mistress's slippery vagina, while her thumb sought out and

worked the swollen little button above, rubbing it this way
and that.

Molly opened her eyes, for Mistress was making small moans
of distress, or so it sounded. But though a deep frown had
appeared on Lady Granger's otherwise smooth brow, her full
lips wore a marvellous smile; if Molly showed any sign of ceasing
her sensitive manipulations of Mistress's private parts, then
Mistress's slender fingers would clasp Molly's wrist urgently and
press Molly's coarse, work-weathered fingers against her sex by
way of encouragement.

Now it was Lady Granger's turn to redden, her face, her neck
and her upper chest flushed a delicate pink. Her lips ovalled
into an 'O', her eyes, previously half-closed, now stared into
the middle distance and her frown deepened. Molly could
feel the small tremors grow into strong shudders, then body-
wracking contractions that held Molly's hand a prisoner between
Mistress's thighs. Warm water splashed over the edge of the bath
and soaked Molly's white cotton apron.

'Thank you, Molly. That will be all.'

'Yes, M'lady.'

And so it had ended. For that day…

GALLERY VIII

JOHN DUPRET

AN EXTRACT FROM

THE SERVING GIRL

R L MORNINGTON

And so to our last selection. RL Mornington's *The Serving Girl* is a tale of the 21st century Maid, for yes, they do exist. Young Emily takes up the position of housemaid under the autocratic and mysterious 'Sir'. Gradually an intense and highly explicit sexual relationship develops between employer and employee, although the protocol of the Master-maid relationship is strictly adhered to. Everything about this liaison, with its elements of authority and servility, is extraordinary and unexpected.

Emily accompanies Sir on a trip by private jet to an undisclosed destination, possibly somewhere in Spain. Here the Señora's maid, Rosa, meets her. Emily finds that Rosa is a kindred spirit, who provides a Hispanic mirror image of Emily's own position. The Señora and Sir, who already have a sexual history together, are not slow to put their respective maids through their paces.

'Now, Rosa, you know the medicine is for your own good. Without, you are disagreeable.'

Turning to Sir, she said:

'I think I'll save us for a little later. Your first relief can be with my girl here. I know it will be rather too brief for my tastes. No, not now! You will need to wait for the medication to take hold.'

Sir already had hold of Rosa's skirt and had lifted it to reveal first a full and rounded behind and then, as the girl spun around trying to escape, a glimpse of an entirely defoliated pussy, with plump pudenda and a pronounced cleft. Emily tried not to stare. 'So the underwear rules apply here too,' she thought.

'Rosa, don't be disobedient. He wishes to inspect you. I'm sure he can contain himself until you are more relaxed.'

The Señora led Sir away to the fireplace, and they stood

talking for a while, just out of Emily's earshot. Sir remained fully aroused and Emily saw, with the Señora, what she had never seen before – that Sir was quite tender in his actions with her, showing none of the brutal insistence he had shown to Emily or any other woman she had seen him with. It was as if the Señora had him tamed and at that there was a part of Emily that acknowledged disappointment.

To Emily's left, Rosa was breathing hard, apparently cursing under her breath in her own language. The dark eyes that had seemed so calm, so calming earlier, now blazed with anger. But as Emily watched, this fire died and Rosa's gaze reverted to vacancy, a fixed and glazed stare into the middle distance. She slumped a little, staggered forward and Emily moved to catch her. The Señora turned from Sir, whose fingers were still occupied on her breasts.

'She's ready now, I think.'

Sir moved quickly across the room, undoing his belt and opening his trousers as he went. He took Rosa by the elbow and hurried her towards the sofa. The Señora sat down on the edge of an armchair opposite, an expectant spectator.

Sir began to arrange Rosa to his liking, on her back, with her crotch at the very edge of the seat. The girl seemed to return to her senses and as he began to manoeuvre himself into position, she squirmed and kicked. Rosa brought her hands to between her legs to protect herself from Sir's cock, which, now free of his trousers, seemed to spring forward of him, a little dribble of fluid already forming at its tip. Rosa shrieked, while Sir tried to pull her hands away from her crotch. The Señora, who had lolled back in the chair and begun to masturbate, barked at Emily:

'Girl! Assist your master!'

Dumbly, obediently, Emily went to do as she was told. After some wrestling, she sat behind Rosa and pulled the other maid's arms behind her. Rosa still bucked and writhed, but no longer shouted. As Sir made his initial entry she whimpered a little, then fell silent. The fight had obviously inspired him, for he settled on a rhythm of long strokes, hard thrusts that jolted Rosa's increasingly inert body. Emily let her arms free, but discreetly held one of her hands, gently caressing the fingers and maintaining what she hoped was a reassuring physical presence. Did she imagine it, or was there a brief responding pressure on her fingers, an acknowledgement of her presence from the otherwise apparently insensate person lodged between her legs?

The Señora continued to masturbate, staring at Sir's body working away at that of the maid beneath him. Rosa's head bounced in Emily's lap, and she could feel that her skirt was being pressed into her own wetness, not only the sweat in which she was now thoroughly bathed, but also the stickier substance oozing from her crotch. Guiltily she realised the extent to which she was sharing the Señora's fascination with this scene. Sir's movements quickened and, his hips slapping hard against Rosa's thighs, he achieved his ejaculation.

Sir withdrew and the Señora left her seat to hug and kiss him. She knelt down and took as much of Sir's still determinedly rigid penis into her mouth as she could. Satisfied that she had cleaned it of semen, she then turned to inspect Rosa, who was now completely unconscious. Parting the girl's thighs a little wider the Señora put her mouth to the naked, reddened, opened pussy, clamping her lips over the labia. From what Emily could see she was working her tongue vigorously at the inner opening. However, this was to prove to have been more of a sucking than a probing activity, because the Señora then pulled away, with her lips pressed tightly together in a mischievous little grin, and hovered over Emily as if to kiss her: then squirted a copious mouthful of Sir's semen into Emily's face, covering her lips, her chin and one cheek with the white goo.

Sir, delighted by this use of his fluid, became animated again, eagerly grabbing at the Señora, attempting to turn her over, to fuck her.

'No! Not yet. I want stimulation of another kind. No, not you, a female knows how to do this best.'

Emily realised the Señora was looking at her. Somehow she had instantly understood what the woman was referring to. Before Emily was able to protest (she'd never done this before, she didn't know how...), Sir had taken her by the hair and pulled her head down to the Señora's waiting, sopping crotch. She was confronted with something familiar yet different – memories of what she had seen in scraps of pornographic magazines shredded in the woods behind her house, her own explorations with a small handbag mirror... And now this, an oozing pussy, its labia swollen and an angry red, the clitoris overt above.

There could really be no technique, no special trick to it. Yet still, Emily hesitated and was instantly reminded of her duty by the gentle pressure of Sir's cock resting flat against the crease of her buttocks, a silent warning of what punishment might be forthcoming if she did not perform what was required of her. Of course, Sir's favoured form of chastisement was no longer quite so traumatic, and on occasion and in spite of herself, Emily yearned for it, even sought it. But she would not be sodomised in front of this strange woman. So Emily dutifully began to use her tongue in an empathic approximation of cunnilingus.

Emily obviously had it right for the Señora was moaning softly, fingers tangling in the English maid's hair and a palm resting gently on her head. As Emily moved back to take a breath she saw the aperture below her mouth opening spasmodically, drooling a little whitish moisture quite similar to Sir's. Sir himself was also evidently pleased. With subtle dexterity he had moved his cock down and was slowly inserting it now into Emily's pussy. She gasped, but she was well lubricated and Sir rode in easily until his pubic hair rubbed at her buttocks. She returned her tongue to its now established rhythm, while Sir found his, slow and gentle lest he disturb her work at the other end of her body.

In the end, Emily was only vaguely aware of her success at her first oral stimulation of another woman, as the greater part of her consciousness was concerned with at once enjoying Sir's movements inside her and suppressing betrayal of this enjoyment. Not only was the smell and taste of cunt, though not conventionally pleasant, significantly arousing, but Sir's final thrusts and subsequent pulsing ejaculation had her straining to defy involuntary expression of her feelings.

Though it could not be evinced from Emily's countenance, she felt profound gratitude when the Señora repeated on her what she had previously done with Rosa, feeling the woman's mouth hungrily sucking at her, then positively bathed in the liquid thus extracted with a second warm splashing of her face and now her neck. Shoved rudely aside onto the floor beside the other, comatose maid, her face resting in a thick puddle of come, her vagina tightened and throbbing, she slipped into a reverie of her own as Sir was finally allowed his Señora.

INDEX OF PICTURES

If you enjoyed the images in this book, you may like the following:

The Secret Art of
Tom Poulton

Over 160 drawings of some of the most graphic and unusual sex we've ever printed. With two novellas.
£18.95

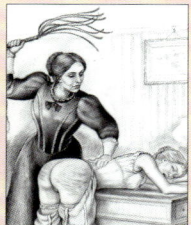

Painful Pleasures
Lynn Paula Russell

Pleasure through pain. 150 brand new, achingly erotic images from an incredible artist.
£19.95

A Sexual Odyssey
Lynn Paula Russell

Russell writes of her journey of sexual discovery. Accompanied by a huge number of her images.
£19.95

The Serving Girl
R L Mornington

Beautiful and innocent Emily takes up the position of housemaid under the autocratic and mysterious 'Sir'.
£7.95

Fireside Orgies
Tom Sargent

Sargent's exquisite vision of a very British way of life and the sexual beings who populate it.
£19.95

Fuck Fashion
Ben Westwood

For the first time, Westwood makes his more explicit images available to the public. A controversial hit.
£19.95

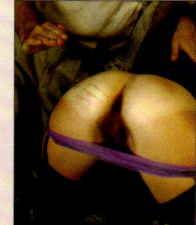

SPANK!
Eric Wilkins

One of our most popular photographers, Wilkins' latest book focuses on the world of spanking.
£19.95

Dark Sex
DuPret

Perhaps the finest collection of early 20th century fetish photography ever assembled.
£18.99

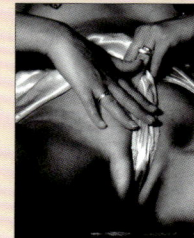

The Cabinet of Dark Things
China Hamilton

The biggest and finest collection of this amazing photographer's erotic images.
£19.95

Lost Drawings
Tom Poulton

A must-have for any lover of this superb erotic artist's work. With a wicked underground novella.
£18.95

THE SCARLET LIBRARY

At the Erotic Print Society, we think that books can and should be decently made. That is why we created the Scarlet Library: the most sensuous and shamelessly erotic books available today, beautifully illustrated by the finest contemporary artists.

Prices range from £12.95 to £14.95

Beatrice
GORDON GRIMLEY

with new illustrations by
LYNN PAULA RUSSELL

The Simple Tale of Susan Aked
ANONYMOUS

with new illustrations by
CHRIS PRICE

Eveline
ANONYMOUS

with new illustrations by
VANIA ZOURAVLIOV

Summer in the Country
AUGUSTE POULET-MALASSIS

with new illustrations by
ADRIAN GEORGE

Gamiani
ALFRED DE MUSSET

with new illustrations by
VANIA ZOURAVLIOV

Two Flappers in Paris
ANONYMOUS

with new illustrations by
SOPHIE ALEXANDER

Letters from a Friend in Paris
ANONYMOUS

with new illustrations by
MICHAEL FARADAY

A Weekend Visit
ANONYMOUS

with new illustrations by
TIM MAJOR

A Night in a Moorish Harem
ANONYMOUS

with illustrations by
HARRY DOUGLAS

The Way of a Man with a Maid
ANONYMOUS

with new illustrations by
TIM MAJOR

Fanny Hill
VOLUME I
JOHN CLELAND

with new illustrations by
ERICH VON GÖTHA

Fanny Hill
VOLUME II
JOHN CLELAND

with new illustrations by
ERICH VON GÖTHA